FIFTY SHADES OF SNOW 2

Lock Down Publications and Ca$h

Presents

Fifty Shades of Snow 2
A Novel by **A. Roy Milligan**

Lock Down Publications
Po Box 944
Stockbridge, Ga 30281

Visit our website @

www.lockdownpublications.com

Copyright by A. Roy Milligan

Fifty Shades of Snow 2

Lock Down Publications

Like our page on Facebook: Lock Down Publications @

www.facebook.com/lockdownpublications.ldp

Stay Connected with Us!

Text **LOCKDOWN** to 22828 to stay up-to-date with new releases,

sneak peaks, contests and more...

Thank you.

Submission Guideline.

Submit the first three chapters of your completed manuscript to ldpsubmissions@gmail.com, subject line: Your book's title. The manuscript must be in a .doc file and sent as an attachment. Document should be in Times New Roman, double spaced and in size 12 font. Also, provide your synopsis and full contact information. If sending multiple submissions, they must each be in a separate email.

Have a story but no way to send it electronically? You can still submit to LDP/Ca$h Presents. Send in the first three chapters, written or typed, of your completed manuscript to:

LDP: Submissions Dept
Po Box 944
Stockbridge, Ga 30281

DO NOT send original manuscript. Must be a duplicate.

Provide your synopsis and a cover letter containing your full contact information.

Thanks for considering LDP and Ca$h Presents.

CHAPTER
ONE

Angelia jumped so hard she nearly fell off the bed. She had beads of sweat all over her neck and forehead that ran down the side of her face. As she looked around the room, nobody was there besides Jon Jon snoring with his mouth wide open. Angelia used to always tease Jon Jon about his snoring. He always denied that he snored until she took a video of him with her phone. When she showed it to him, he saw himself laying there snoring loud as hell. After that, he stopped trying to deny it.

The liquor was strong on his breath from last night, and she knew that he was out of it. She also knew he wouldn't notice her movements. She glanced at the clock sitting on the marble top night stand and noticed that it was 7 am so she laid back down, realizing she was in a dream that felt so real it left her heart beating as if she had just gotten done running. She covered back up, got closer to Jon Jon, put one of her legs on his, and rubbed his chest.

She soon made her way down to his dick where she noticed it was hard as a rock. She smiled and pulled the decorative comforter back. She got on all fours and her eyes traced from his jawline, to his chest, past his midsection, and came to a stop at his rock hard soldier, standing at full attention. Jon Jon was out like a light, but

Angelia knew he wouldn't mind if she used his swollen member for her own personal pleasure. She slowly wrapped her fingers around the base of his dick, smiled, and slowly licked it from the base to the tip. She paused when she got to the tip, and exhaled slowly as she opened her mouth and wrapped her soft lips around the head. Suddenly, she quickly slid her lips all the way back down to the base of his dick, moving her hand up and down to stroke it. She slid her mouth back to the tip, firmly reattaching her fingers around the base. Her panties were immediately soaked. *I need this dick inside me*, she thought to herself.

Angelia got on her knees, straddling Jon Jon, and reached down grabbing his still rock hard dick. She began to rub his tip around on her pussy lips, and the juices began to roll down his dick. She sat down all the way, and his dick filled her up perfectly. She felt the pressure against her cervix, and although it was slightly uncomfortable, she let her hips drop down even further.

"Oh, fuck," she whispered quietly although she didn't really care if Jon Jon woke up. It only took her about six minutes to make herself cum, and she collapsed, asleep on top of him.

Steve had just left James' house. They had been playing the video game where Steve lost $400 in Madden, as usual. James was always winning, but Steve would never give up. James was also showing him his grow set up and explaining the new strains to him that he had just received from Colorado.

James had recently took down his grow tents in the basement after his last harvest, and built rooms for cloning and mother plants, vegetative growth, flowering, and drying. He had installed high end carbon filters with inline fans so there was no smell at all in the house until you opened up one of the rooms. Steve could tell that James really took pride in what he was doing with those plants. James knew everything there was about his new grow operation, but was still always reading books to learn more. For James, it was more than a hobby; it was a passion. "And that's why I stopped using the ProMix HP, which is a peat based, soilless mix with perlite, which is puffed volcanic glass, and moved to a straight coco coir growing medium. It allows me to get the same, if not a greater yield, using less growing medium and smaller pots," James said, smiling.

"Bro, I don't know what exactly you just said, but it sounds like you're really starting to know your shit," Steve said. Steve was honestly impressed. James had tried to get Steve to sit and listen to him about his grow set up in the past, but Steve finally took the time today to sit there for a few hours while James educated him.

CHAPTER
TWO

Steve headed to Juice's house, calling him once he arrived and Juice came running out, getting inside the car. "What's up, bro? Please tell me something good. You done gave me some good bricks for a good price, now all these niggas calling back trying to get this shit. They loving this shit. Please tell me something good, bro." Juice was staring at Steve in anticipation.

Steve smiled. It was like music to his ears to hear Juice happy about the product he had given him.

"I'm thinking, maybe Tuesday. I would say tomorrow, but I can say for sure Tuesday. How many you thinking you going to want?" Steve asked, hoping that Juice would want at least a few.

Juice scratched his head and nodded, thinking about what he could realistically handle considering how good the quality was compared to what anyone else in the city had. "As long as it's the same or just as good, bro, I'ma say like 5 for sure. That's like every 3 days though, bro. Once I collect all my money out the street, I'll be grabbing some more. I'd rather get that shit from you, at least I know I'm getting the right shit. These niggas be playing so many games out here with that shit, it's frustrating. And the dude I was dealing with in Detroit, he never have shit consistently. He would have 15, 20 bricks today, and in a few days, he ain't got none."

"Damn. See that's what I'm trying to figure out. I want to have it where I never run out and we can keep shit flowing," Steve said, knowing that was what Juice clearly wanted to have happen too.

"Trust me, I can move your whole bag once I get to flowing and niggas can see I got it consistent. I'm good for 10 a week for sure once that happens, if not more."

"So if I start really getting this shit, you can move 10 a week?" Steve asked him in a serious tone. He wanted to make sure that he wasn't getting his hopes up for nothing.

"Hell yea! Easy! That's just starting. I'd buy 10 right now if I had all my money pulled out the streets," Juice exclaimed looking Steve dead in the eyes to let him know he wasn't playing.

Steve thought to himself for a second while Juice was talking. He was looking out the window at the sky daydreaming while thinking about all the money he would be making. "I'ma see what I can do," Steve replied, not wanting to promise something that he wasn't sure he could pull off.

"It sounds like you got access. Don't be scared of a big load. I got niggas everywhere. I'll move that shit for you, all of it. Especially right now. It's a drought right now, and all these niggas dope is cut up, for real. If you get this shit consistent, it wouldn't even be competition because I'm not stepping on the shit like the rest of these niggas out here. People very happy with what I'm giving them, no complaints. They love it. I got the best shit and the best price and that's why this shit gone fly bro, I'm telling you. These other niggas really trying to cut and stretch their shit too far. It's no comparison with what I'm providing."

"Well, I'ma definitely let you know something in a couple weeks. I'ma see what I can put together, but for now I need your help with some shit. I got like 15 I'm going to go pick up, and all of them yours if you get me paid for them pretty quick."

"Is it the same as last time?"

"I mean, yea, based on who I'm getting this shit from, they not gone play no games. That shit going to be A-1."

"Say less. I'ma come up with some more money, don't worry. I'll be able to cash at least 8 out and as the money coming in, I'll give it straight to you. What kind of price you going to give me?"

"45,000 good?"

"Hell yeah! Niggas charging more than that for some bullshit. That shit be all kind of colors, smelling weird and all. I don't know what these niggas be putting in that shit," he said and they both laughed.

"I don't know what color or shade this shit gone be, but I know it's gone be what you want and what you been looking for. That's what I can guarantee fasho."

They gave each other a pound. "Holla at me as soon as you get them in hand. I'll be waiting for you," Juice said before he got out of the car.

CHAPTER
THREE

Steve then drove off slowly, calculating numbers in his head, heading to his twin cousin's house in Detroit. He saw himself counting a million dollars in all blue hundreds, and that made him smile. He thought about all the things he could do for Angelia that he felt would make her happy. He thought about all the people that had really been there for him, holding him down over the years. It felt good to think about all the things he could do for them.

The twin cousins he was on his way to meet were his cousins on his dad's side. They were from the hood, 22 years old and they rapped and sold drugs. They were always dressed up in expensive designer and drove new model cars. It was like every time Steve saw them, they had a new car. When Steve would ask them why they always had new cars, they would just laugh, and talk about how they were addicted to that new car smell. His aunt, who was their mom, was never at home. All she did was hustle, running lottery numbers all through the hood. She was gone of course once he arrived and he saw both of them on the porch. It looked like they were going back and forth rapping in a small cypher. They noticed Steve as soon as he pulled in the driveway. "Nigga, what happened to your rims? Don't tell me a nigga done stole your shit!"

Steve laughed, "Naw, I took them hot ass rims off. Fuck that shit. I'm trying to be low key. You trying to buy them or something?"

"Yea, how much you want for them? I'll cash you out right now," one of the twins said as he pulled out a wad of money and started pulling hundred dollar bills off. Both twins were identical, brown skin, stood 5 ft. tall with dreads and they both favored the rapper King Von, rest in peace to the young talented rapper. The only difference between the twins was that one of them had a scar on the side of his face.

"$500 and you can have them," Steve said.

"Bet. When you want me to come get them?" Drew asked, holding his pants up in the front. He was the one with the scar on his face.

"We can set something up this week. Y'all can come down and holla at me. What y'all been up to?"

"Shit, for real, just getting this money out here. You see this shit, nigga," Dior said, showing his money off and smiling.

"Nigga, that ain't shit. That ain't no money. You ain't even buying a brick yet, are you?"

Drew and Dior looked at each other and started laughing. "You got us fucked up! We got the bricks," Dior said.

"Oh, y'all got the bricks? How much for one?"

"About $49,000 for you, and it's some of the best shit around."

"How much you paid for it?"

"Honestly . . . I'm paying $48,500, but that's only because I'm buying one. I'm only taxing you $500."

"I thought you just said y'all got the bricks? Cappin' ass niggas," Steve said, laughing while shaking his head. The twins laughed as well and were speechless. "Nigga, y'all be selling that shit out y'all momma house? Where y'all lay at?"

"Hell fuck naw! Moms will flush all that shit down the toilet if she found that shit. She ain't having that shit. Nigga, we got spots set up and we got niggas that be going to West Virginia and back with the duffle bags. We only here at the crib because you said you wanted to pull up. We both know you ain't want to be pulling up in the slums where wild shit be happening."

Steve laughed. "You right about that."

CHAPTER
FOUR

H is cousins always looked up to him and admired him a lot, but Steve never really made time for them. They never did him wrong in any way, Steve just always had his own stuff going on over the years. Steve always had a job, a girl, and some kind of side hustle going on. He loved his little cousins, but just always had other stuff happening that kept him busy. After Steve talked to his Uncle Swift last time, he told him that it would be cool to deal with them on some business and that he didn't have to worry about Drew and Dior not being solid. Steve knew they were in the street hustling and they always had new cars, flashy jewelry, and a lot of females. Although they were hustlers, they didn't play games. They both kept a gun at all times and weren't afraid to use it.

Some people liked to keep a gun just to say they had one. When it came to Drew and Dior though, they were not the ones to play with. They had built a solid reputation for themselves over the years, and were well respected, despite their young age.

"So what if I can get y'all bricks at $35,000? What y'all can do with them?"

"Fuck you mean? Nigga, we gone take over this bitch! We will run through all that you got! For $35,000, we gone be rich as fuck! I know plenty of niggas that will buy bricks. Even if we gotta off them at $40,000, they gone fly," Dior said, getting excited.

"Stop playing with us. You driving this weak ass Impala talking about you can give us bricks for $35,000. I don't think you know what you taking about," Drew told him.

"The car I'm driving don't mean shit. See, that's what's wrong with you young niggas coming up. Y'all think just because a nigga ain't driving a nice car, he's broke."

"I'm just saying, you sitting here talking about you can give us bricks for the cheapest price in Detroit. What you den hit a lick or something?" Drew said, crossing his arms.

"Relax. You talking like the shit impossible or something. I'm just telling you what I can do for you. You want it or not?"

"Nigga, I'm in. Fuck this nigga," Dior said as he waved his hand as if shooing someone away.

"I'm in too. I'm just saying, I have to see it to believe it."

"Don't worry about that part. You just worry about how many you going to be able to move a week so I can make sure I get enough to always keep the flow smooth and you don't run out."

Drew and Dior both wanted to be excited about the thought of getting bricks for that price, but they weren't sure if Steve could pull it off. One thing they both had come to understand is that a lot of people talk a big game, but a lot less people actually follow through with what they say.

Later that day, Steve went and got a stash spot in his car so he could ride with drugs at will with less worry. He went and got all the cut from the guy his uncle sent him to, which took longer than he thought it would. He had no clue who Steve was and gave him a hard time until he felt comfortable. He sent Steve on his way and told him to tell his uncle hello and if he needed anything else, to just drop by. Steve then deposited $5,000 in Swift's prison account. Now all he was waiting for was his new delivery.

CHAPTER
FIVE

Angelia and Jon Jon were on the plane, on their way back to Michigan. They were now sitting in regular seats since they gave their first class seats up to senior citizens who were both walking with canes. The seats they were sitting in were still comfortable, especially since they were sitting in the row by themselves. They couldn't keep their hands off each other. Jon Jon had had a few drinks and he couldn't keep his hand from under her dress. At first, Angelia was nervous, but after she had just one shot of vodka, she loosened up and started to let him have his way. She was no longer worried about the other passengers on the plane. That little bit of vodka, along with Jon Jon's touch, made her forget about everything else at the moment. He kept kissing her, sticking his tongue nearly down her throat. She wanted to pull him inside one of the bathrooms for a couple minutes.

"You going to be my wife right?" he asked while still kissing her and nibbling on her ear.

"Yes," she said as she felt her juices flowing. Jon Jon always knew how to get her going.

"Say it," Jon Jon whispered into her ear while pressing his cheek softly against hers.

"I'm going to be your wife, Papi," she said before he started tongue kissing her again. They had a small blanket they were sharing, and Jon Jon's hands were creeping slowly under her dress. He traced his finger gently up the inside of her leg until his fingers were inside her wet hole. She was soaking wet so he added a second finger.

"Damn you wet."

He kissed her slowly while working his fingers inside her as he listened to her moans and felt how her body was trembling every time he reached a certain spot. "I wonder if I can make you cum," he whispered.

"Mm, probably, but my dress gone be all messed up, so no," she said smiling and gently trying to move his hands.

"You can tell I love this pussy, huh?"

"I guess so," Angelia said while slightly shrugging her shoulders and making a cute face at him.

"I do. What you mean, you guess? I will kill a nigga over this pussy. This gone be my pussy. I don't know what you waiting for." He took his fingers out and his hands were all soaked with her juices. He started licking it all off with his vicious tongue. "I love the way you taste," he said passionately.

She smiled and started back kissing him. She always felt like no one was around when she was with him. She never paid attention to who was watching or listening. It didn't matter to her because she never felt embarrassed with him. It was like the whole world stopped for her when they were together.

CHAPTER
SIX

S oon, the flight attendant came over the speaker and told everyone that they only had 30 minutes left before they were arriving to Detroit, Michigan.

"That was fast," Angelia said, beginning to fix herself up. She had made a mess and most likely would have to tie the small blanket around her once they got off the plane.

"I got a question," Jon Jon stated.

"Yes, Papi?"

"How much your dude be getting them bricks of white for?"

"I'm not sure. I don't even think they are his. He don't have money like that. Honestly, I think they are for his uncle, the one that's locked up in the Feds. He was a big drug dealer I guess once upon a time."

"Find out for me. It's a drought out here and prices through the roof. You have family in Michigan right? Like a cousin?" Jon Jon asked as he stretched his arms over his head and groaned. Even though the seat was not terrible, he was glad they were landing soon so he could get up and stretch out his legs.

"No, I don't? Why you asked?"

"Just trying to see who you can tell him you are inquiring for so he won't be looking at you all skeptical."

"Oh, that's easy. My dad used to mess around back in the day so I can just use him. He knows my dad and he always jokes with him about getting back in the game."

"Oh, so your dad used to be the bird man back in the day? Why he stop?" Jon Jon asked curiously.

"Yes. He used to have so much of it, but it's a long story. We basically had to move away and run for our lives because the cartel my dad was working for didn't want him to stop, but my mom was tired of all the violence that came with it. She basically told him, you have all this money, how much is enough? It's the family or you continue to be greedy. My dad thought about it. She was right. He had everything he wanted. There was no good reason for him to keep going any more, so he stopped and that's when they came for us. They were trying to kill us, so we had to do all kinds of stuff just to get away."

"Damn, that's crazy. That shit really serious like that, huh. You know we hear about that kind of shit on the TV, like when if you try to stop, they want to kill you and your family."

"No, it's real. The TV is telling the truth."

"That's a fucked up situation."

"It's a way of life where I came from."

"Damn, I hear you. I'm glad you survived it. Just let me know the prices though, ASAP. I'm just curious. Although it may not even be on my level, I had to ask. You know how I am. I'm always trying to use my resources, because you never know." Angelia knew Jon Jon was definitely a resourceful person. He had a lot of contacts, and knew who to call and for what.

She giggled. "It's ok. You know I got you, but what do you mean it may not be on your level?" Angelia asked while squinting her eyes at him a little.

"Like price and quality. I get solid shit at a nice price, but shit kinda messed up right now, so let me know as soon as you can."

"Ok. I can do that, Papi," she said as she pecked him on the lips. She smiled when she saw Esha walking past at a fast pace on the way to the bathroom. "Your bathroom up there," Angelia said.

"Somebody in there taking forever. I'm not about to pee on myself. I have to go now," Esha said.

Angelia giggled as she watched her speed walking down the aisle.

CHAPTER
SEVEN

Soon they landed and Angelia and Esha left together.

"We have to do that more often," Angelia said.

"YOU need to do it more often. You know damn well I stay getting flewed out somewhere. I've been telling your ass forever but you don't be listening to me," Esha said with a smirk on her face.

Angelia giggled. "I know, I know. I didn't realize how much fun I was missing. Trust me, I woulda been in the air with you. Steve don't ever want to go nowhere or do anything. It was cool at first, but now it's getting old. I don't want to miss my best years sitting in the house. He like an old man. He just want to work and save money," Angelia said while tossing up her hands into the air.

Esha giggled. "He just bought you a car. A Cadillac at that. So he musta been saving for a reason. Your ass just in love with Jon Jon, that's all."

They both cracked up.

"That is not true!"

"Had your ass screaming like you was getting raped," Esha joked.

"Shut up! I was not that loud."

"I ran in there. You was so loud. I'm like, what the hell. You was real loud. I had to see what was going on. A bitch got nervous." They both giggled.

"Jon Jon talking about going to Jamaica soon. You coming?" Angelia asked.

"You know I'm in. The real question is, are you coming? Or can you come? Steve gone flip out on your ass. See, you playing with fire. You might as well just leave the nigga. You know Jon Jon gone get you a place and everything."

"I know, but I want to have my own money. Dudes be extra when they paying rent and all that, and I know Jon Jon is one of them types. I need to save up my own money if I'm going to leave, but I'm not sure I want to leave. I love Steve."

Esha shook her head.

"What? I'm just having a little fun right now, that's all. I still don't know if I want to be with Jon Jon 100 percent yet," Angelia added.

"Who dick the best?"

"Jon Jon's for sure, for sure," Angelia said with certainty.

"I'll have to leave," Esha said and they both bust out in laughter.

Angelia had been texting Steve the whole way home and they were telling each other how much they were missing each other. As soon as Angelia came through the door, there were flowers, balloons, and rose pedals all over the place. All she saw was red and pink. Her mouth dropped as she noticed the place looking like a garden. "Oh my god!" she said as she turned red in the face. She gave Steve a big hug and kissed him on the lips. She looked up the staircase and noticed the rose pedals led up there too.

"How was your trip, boo?" Steve asked while smiling at her.

"It was fun. It's cool getting away for a second. I needed that. Wish you coulda come with us."

"I know. I'm sorry, boo. You know I woulda went if I could have."

"Next time," she said, walking up the steps and noticing he had a nice, hot bubble bath waiting for her. There were relaxing scented candles all around. "Just what I needed."

"I figured you would appreciate a hot bath after touching down from that long plane trip," Steve said while clasping her hand with his and looking into her eyes.

"Yes, for sure. Thank you, baby." She kissed him again. He did notice that she kind of smelled like a man's cologne, but he thought nothing serious about it. He was just ready to lay down so he could get up in the morning. He had received a text from the phone Karo gave him telling him 8 AM. He laid in bed trying to wait for Angelia to come to bed, but she took her time in the bath, texting Jon Jon for over an hour, so Steve fell asleep waiting for her.

CHAPTER
EIGHT

He had been at his mom's since 7 a.m., when he saw a flat bed pull up with a Chrysler mini van. The man let it down right in front of where Steve was standing. He had Steve sign the delivery slip and then he gave him a yellow envelope containing the title, keys and invoice and left. Steve soon got a text saying to look inside the glove compartment and that's where he found a small paper that told him to turn the vehicle to 'on' push the gas pedal 5 times, brake one, gas pedal twice, then hit the right blinker. As he followed instructions, there was a noise in the back right under the backseat. The note also told him to take the back seat out. As he did, he noticed a hidden compartment that came out the floor, containing a thin bag that was pretty small but, inside, it had all 15 kilos on top of each other and on the side of each other. They were wrapped incredibly well and tight, and there was no scent at all.

Steve was excited. He went and put the bag in his stash spot in his car, and went back in to tell his mom that the van was her new car. It was only 4 years old with 60,000 miles on it, and it was clean as a whistle. It was a nice, dark gunmetal silver. For a mini van, it looked good. Of course, she cried and was so happy about the new car. Her old one had been giving her some issues, and needed a few repairs. She was glad to not have to worry about that anymore. She hugged and kissed him, and told him she would check it out once she put some clothes on. With that said, Steve was heading home. On his way home, he thought about how good it felt to take care of his mom like that. He was a good son, but never really had the means to just up and buy his mom a car like that before.

When Steve got home, he got right to work taking 4 and a half ounces out of each kilo, replacing it with cut, then mixing and compressing them back together. James showed up to help him out. They had a good routine in place now, and were making their way through the kilos efficiently.

"You trying to blow up out here . . . well, you is blowing up out here!" James yelled as he was running the blenders.

"Naw, man, I'm just doing a little something," Steve said as humbly as he could.

"Nigga, you got 15 kilos! This ain't little, my man. These niggas out here barely getting one or two, and they acting like they got the 15 kilos, with all the ice around their necks, and the foreign whips they driving. I know for a fact these niggas ain't got no 15 kilos. Actually, I know for a fact they ain't even got 2 kilos," James said as he took one of the mixed kilos and put it all into the compressor that they had sitting on the table. James was amazed while he helped process this volume of coke. Steve was blowing up fast. Nobody could doubt that.

"You never know," Steve replied, still trying to remain humble.

James laughed, "Trust me . . . niggas ain't got this, bro. You doing your thing." He shook his head in disbelief how quick things were coming together for Steve.

"I'm just trying to stack my shit up. I be kind of scared to spend something until my tab paid. I don't want to mess shit up," Steve said as he tilted his head slightly, smiled, and admired the kilo that James had just put in the compressor.

CHAPTER
NINE

"Good morning," Angelia said as she stood, leaning against the doorway.

"Hey, Ang," James said, looking back over his shoulder, giving her a smile.

"Good morning, boo," Steve said as he looked around and noticed Angelia looking at all the kilos just sitting around the room.

"Dang, you getting more and more," she said, but still didn't believe he was making as much profit as he was. She figured he was just doing some work for Uncle Swift.

Steve smiled. "What you cooking?"

"Whatever you want," Angelia replied, giving him a big grin.

"Pancakes, bacon, eggs. Can you make them one pancakes you be making with the pecans and the bananas?" Steve asked as his stomach growled just from him thinking about those pancakes.

"Got you, Papi," she said while heading down the stairs.

"So what's the difference between the last stuff and this? It seems like it was a darker white tint than these are. These seem whiter. Do that mean it's better or worse?"

"Naw, it be all kind of shades. I'm only able to tell how good it is when I cook it. The last shit was better. Notice how last time I said, take 10 grams of real and 20 grams of cut. This time we mixing a hundred grams at a time in way bigger blenders. It's way faster this time because I'm not cutting it as hard, you know?" Steve explained while turning off one of the blenders.

"Yea, I get it." James said.

"That first time, my uncle had some strong shit," he said laughing. "That nigga probably went to Mexico hisself and got them."

"You mean Colombia . . . That's where that shit really at. Remember Pablo Escobar?"

"I heard of him, I think."

"Bro, what? You need to watch the first season of Narcos and learn something. He was that nigga over there in Colombia."

"I'ma have to check it out."

"I'ma get at you later on. Let me go water these plants and shit."

"Ok, bet."

"Oh, tell me what I should do to get waves again. I remember you said you had the recipe. I be brushing all day. My shit still barely in."

"You gotta wash your hair first about 3 times. On the third time, it's going to be way more soapy. Don't use no cheap shampoo. You need some good shit. So once you lather it up, start to brush in your pattern. Brush until you see it. Make sure it's soapy as fuck though, even if you gotta add more shampoo, that's cool. Grab a durag. This is going to keep your pattern in place. Tie it nice and tight so your waves don't move underneath it. Wash it out while the durag is on your head and let it dry. Don't take your durag off until it's fully dry. Then, like magic, nigga you got waves, that easy."

"Get the fuck out of here. That's for your good hair having ass!" James replied pointing at Steve's head.

"Naw, that's for you. I ain't got to do that . . . try it and see."

"Ok, I'ma check it out and see," he said as he went to the door. "Is this house set up like the last house, or am I tripping?"

"It is kind of, just got an extra room, but yea pretty much," Angelia said.

"That's that Pontiac shit. A lot of cribs are similar . . . Alright, I'll holla at y'all later," James said and went out the door.

CHAPTER
TEN

Minutes later, Steve came down the stairs to the smell of breakfast. Angelia put a plate in front of him and sat down next to him. They both started eating at the table. "What you doing today?"

"I'll be running around for most of the day. Gotta run into a few guys. What you got up?" Steve said as he chewed on a bite of the pecan and banana pancakes and picked up a piece of crispy bacon.

"Me and Candy going to a day party just to support her cousin."

"Oh, ok, ok. In Pontiac or Detroit?" Steve pointed at the food, nodding his head in approval.

"Detroit," Angelia replied, smiling that Steve was happy with what she cooked. "You wanna come with us?"

"Hell naw!" Steve said while laughing. "You know I ain't going to nothing like that. I ain't into that type of shit. I got work to do anyway."

"It's going to be fun. You missing out," she joked.

"Shit, have fun," Steve said as he dipped the last bite of his pancake into syrup.

"My dad wanted to know how much you want for a kilo. He told me not to tell you he wanted it, but I'm not about to not tell you."

Steve laughed. "Tell him $33,000. I won't tax him too much, plus I'll give them to him just how I get them, untouched. You can keep a thousand off each one too."

"Ok, I don't know how good that price is, but I'ma let him know."

"Is he gone be moving a lot of them?"

"Hmmm, I have no idea. I'll let you know later on after I talk to him."

"Ok, cool."

Angelia texted Jon Jon the number and he was trying to call her, but she couldn't answer. He sent a text for her to bring him one. He wanted to check out the quality before he committed to more. He also told her he was going to give her $34,000 if it checks out to be good. Jon Jon was thinking that it sounded too good to be true. She told Steve and he gave her one. Jon Jon kept texting her as if it was an emergency, but little did she know, he had been paying $40-41k, so this was an amazing deal for him as long as the quality was there.

"My mom keep texting me. Can I just bring that to my dad right quick?"

"Yea, go head. Use my car though. I got a stash spot inside. I'll show you how to use it."

"I'm not going to get pulled over. I'll just drive mine. I ain't going far, so I'll be good." She already had Jon Jon coming to Auburn Hills. He was going to grab a hotel there. She was still in her pajamas, tight spandex, pink booty shorts, and a white belly t-shirt. She grabbed a backpack and headed out about 20 minutes later, once she received a text from Jon Jon.

It was a warm but gray and rainy day outside. Angelia got in the front seat, put the address into her phone, and tossed her phone in the cup holder. As she drove down the wet, dirty roads the directions to the hotel came out over the car speakers. She had never been to this hotel before, but had heard of the name. She parked in the parking lot, grabbed her black and white umbrella out of the driver side door compartment, opened it up, and got out of the car. She then walked around to the backside of the car to grab her bag. Her shoes splashed on the wet blacktop as she made her way to the front door. *I hope this place isn't too fancy*, she thought to herself. A guy opened the front door of the hotel, and she collapsed her umbrella, shaking off the rain. When she walked into the lobby of the five star hotel, she noticed how absolutely beautiful it was. It wasn't decorated in the typical modern, sterile fashion of most newer hotels. The lobby had a classic charm. There was a large crystal chandelier hanging from the ceiling and wide, dark wood molding everywhere. Most of the patrons seemed to be wearing suits, dresses, or business attire. Men sat talking in brown leather chairs with briefcases at their sides. Angelia was worried that people might be judging her, because she was underdressed. Luckily, she had such a sexy presence that most of the men in there weren't paying attention to her clothes.

CHAPTER
ELEVEN

T he bellhop, who carried people's bags and took them to their rooms, approached Angelia, and greeted her. "Good afternoon, madam," he said with a smile on his face. "Might you be Angelia? I can take your umbrella and bag if you'd like. I will lead you up to your room. Your host awaits you."

"I'll hang onto my things, thank you. I appreciate it though," Angelia said, giving him a smile back.

"Right this way," he said as he motioned for her to come into the elevator. He pressed the button for the top floor. Even the elevator was nice. Old, dark, well-polished wood lined the walls, and the doors had a classic brass tone to them. The doors opened and the bellhop led her out into what looked like a small lobby area with only one door. It was then that Angelia realized Jon Jon had got the presidential suite.

"I can take it from here, thanks," Angelia said. The bellhop stepped back into the elevator and the doors closed. She knocked on the solid wood door. Jon Jon opened the door to reveal an absolutely stunning suite. It had a living room, kitchen, bedroom and everything. The room was like a whole house. Everything in there was clearly of very high quality. The walls were a deep navy blue, and heavy white curtains adorned the large windows. The dark wood kitchen table and chairs looked like they were from the early 1900's, but were in excellent condition and well polished. "This is nice," she said, noticing some bags Jon Jon had laying there with all his utensils inside. Jon Jon took her bag and umbrella and set them on the brown and cream speckled granite kitchen counter. He had an older white man there standing off to the side. He was a driver Jon Jon used when moving money and drugs around. The man was dressed in khaki pants, with a white button down shirt, brown leather belt and dress shoes. He looked to be in his 50's, clean shaven with a high and tight haircut. He looked professional, but not over the top.

"What's up, baby?" he said kissing her and smacking her ass. "Damn, that ass so fat."

She smiled, a little embarrassed.

Jon Jon pulled the kilo out of the backpack, started cutting up the packaging, and unwrapped it. As soon as he opened it, he already knew it was good. He saw the stamp and knew it was the real deal. The smell was overpowering. "Damn, that nigga got a real plug, huh? This straight from the cartel fasho," he said, tasting it on his finger. His tongue went numb right away. "Try this," he told the white man. He crushed some up, did two lines, and was immediately super high. Both of his eyes widened and he had a big grin across his face.

"Oh yeah, that's that good shit right there!"

"Where he be getting this shit from?" Jon Jon asked Angelia.

"I don't know for sure. I think he gets it from his uncle."

"Damn. Can you get 10 of these, like today?" Jon Jon inquired. The enthusiasm and hope could be heard in his voice and seen in his eyes.

CHAPTER
TWELVE

Angelia texted Steve. He told her that he could sell 3 more until next week, but he would get more sooner if he could. "He said you can buy 3 more. He will be able to get more soon, like in a few days or something."

"Shit, go get them. Here," Jon Jon started counting out the money. He had stacks of hundreds. "This your $4,000. I told you I'll give you $1,000 for each one."

"Thank you. Dang, that was easy," Angelia replied with a smile.

Jon Jon laughed. "Here this $33,000 for this one, and this $99,000 for the other 3. You can take all of it. I know you ain't gone run off."

They all laughed.

"So do the nigga make money? I know he ain't getting this shit that cheap and driving that old ass car. He might just be a work horse for his uncle."

"I . . . I'm not sure. I don't think he makes that much. He just got me that Cadillac, but I think he pays the note. I don't know what he makes, honestly. I ain't seen him having kilos like this before though. He be having handfuls of ounces here and there, but recently, something changed."

"I was just asking, because he getting a good price on these," Jon Jon said casually, while trying to continue to hide the truth that he had never gotten close to a price this good on the real deal before, especially in a drought.

"Yeah, I don't know. Let me go get the rest. I have to start getting ready for the day party," Angelia said as she placed the cash in the backpack and zipped it up.

"Oh we going to that together. You rolling with me. I just bought that new 550 Benz. I need my wifey on the passenger side or in the driver seat, pick one," Jon Jon said as he put his hand on Angelia's shoulder and looked into her eyes.

"Driver seat," she said, excited to be able to drive.

"Before you go, come here for a minute." He pulled her into the bathroom. Jon Jon closed the door behind him. The entire bathroom was a caramel colored marble with glass shower doors. There was a large, long mirror with his and hers sinks underneath. Jon Jon leaned himself back on the sink, pulled his dick out, and pulled down Angelia's shorts. "Suck this dick," he said, pushing her head down, dropping her to her knees. She began sucking until his dick was sticking straight out. "Get up," he said as he grabbed her arm. "Put one leg on the sink." Angelia did as he said. She liked how direct he was when it came to sex. As he slid his dick in and out, he started stroking her pussy and pulling her hair from the middle of her scalp. She had her leg up on the cold marble sink, while looking at Jon Jon behind her in the mirror.

"Oh, Papi! Oh, Papi! Oh! Oh!" she shouted as he pounded her from the back, slamming his dick in and out of her until he came inside her.

"This pussy 20 times better without a condom."

"I'm glad you came, because my leg was shaking about to give out," she said, giggling.

She sat on the toilet and got his nut out of her. She walked out of the bathroom, grabbed her backpack and umbrella, thanked Jon Jon and his driver, and left the hotel room. She got out into the hallway, and pushed the button for the elevator. The doors opened and she was greeted again by the bellhop.

"Leaving already, miss?"

"Yes. This hotel is beautiful. I've never been here before," she said as the elevator came to a stop on the first floor.

"Thank you. We have many repeat guests here. Would you like me to pull your car up for you? It's still raining outside."

"No, thank you. I have my umbrella," Angelia said as she made her way toward the front door of the lobby.

"I hope you enjoyed your visit," he said, noticing that several of the men in business suits couldn't help but stare at Angelia's butt as she walked out the door.

CHAPTER
THIRTEEN

She headed home, feeling great. She made money and got some good dick. She wasn't going to tell Steve she was getting money off it both ways. She had already made plans to buy her a couple Louie purses. She brought back $132,000 and Steve gave her $4,000. She was feeling herself. The outfit she was wearing today to the day party wasn't making it. She was going straight to the mall after she dropped Jon Jon's drugs off.

Steve wound up having 12 more kilos. After he stretched everything he had. Juice had been calling and Shila had been texting and calling him since yesterday. She had left voicemails and all. Steve was starting to feel like what she was doing wasn't working. He didn't like her blowing up his phone all day when he was trying to get things done.

As Steve was on the way to drop 8 kilos off to Juice, he called Shila.

"Dang, I see I got to start making appointments to talk to you," she said.

He laughed. "Naw, I just been busy as hell. Sorry about that."

"I guess my pussy ain't good enough, huh?" Shila replied in a sarcastic tone.

"Chill out. What you up to?"

"Missing you. Getting ready to go to this day party in a little while."

"Where at?"

"Detroit. You going?"

"No, I think Angelia going though."

"Oh, I figured them hoes going to be there."

"Who's party is it?" he asked.

"This dude Kamozy. He a couple years older than us. He be rapping and stuff. I think he just signed a record deal too. He pretty good. You heard of him?"

"Oh, ok. Naw, I never heard of him. Who you going with?"

"My girls. It's about 5 of us. We bouta go there and shut it down, you know," Shila joked while giggling.

"Let me hit you once I'm done handling my business," Steve said as he thought about the few things he needed to get done today.

"Ok. You better call me back. I'll answer even if I'm at the party."

"Ok."

He had just arrived at Juice's house. He was pulling into the driveway, going all the way to the back. Steve was trying to keep it as low key as possible. He didn't want to be seen coming in with a duffle bag and leaving with one anymore. *Small mistakes can have big consequences,* Steve thought to himself. He grabbed the bag out of the stash spot, and climbed the stairs to the back door of the brick home. He knocked three times on the black steel security door. Juice opened the inner door within seconds. He had seen Steve pulling in on the cameras.

CHAPTER

FOURTEEN

hat's good, bro?" Juice smiled from ear to ear, clearly happy to see Steve's face again.

"Chillin, chillin. What's good?" Steve said, handing him the duffle bag and walking inside.

Juice had the money all over the glass table for him along with a money counter. The bills were already stacked into neat piles for Steve to run through the counter. The room smelled like freshly washed laundry, almost like a clean linen candle. The white tile floor in the kitchen was spotless. There wasn't anything on the countertops but a knife block filled with high end knives sitting next to the stainless steel gas range. The kitchen had the set up and space that any amateur chef would love to have in their home, but it didn't look like the kitchen was used too often for cooking food.

Steve ran the money through and it came to $360,000 on the nose. Steve couldn't help but love the sound of the money as it made its way through the counter. *I could get used to that sound*, he thought to himself.

"I'ma be calling you again soon, bro. Gone ahead and get that shit. I'm locked in with you. I got niggas taking this shit out of town and everything. So I'ma just be coming with as much money as I can. That way you can keep getting it."

"Ok, I got you. Just hit me up when you need more," Steve said while giving Juice a pound.

"Oh, I got somebody for you, too. I wanted to hit her, but she know I ain't shit. She got her shit together too, no kids, about 26," Juice explained.

"Who?"

"You know her, too. Aliyah," Juice said with a grin.

"Ouu, shit. I been wanting her forever. That was my high school crush. She was in like 4 of my classes. I been wanting her. She was bad as hell back then. She still looking good these days?"

Juice laughed while nodding his head up and down. "That's my baby momma little cousin. I told her I was gone give you her number. She always be out at my house. You know I got a big dumb ass house on Williams Lake out in Waterford. All you got to do is come out there. She always be coming through."

"I might have to do that. Give her my number. I'll see if she calls."

Juice laughed. "She said the same thing. Just give her a call and be like, Juice told me to call you. How you been? Go from there."

"So she still badd then?"

"Bro, she cold as hell! Light skin, pretty long hair, still looking like Alicia Keys."

They both laughed. Steve could picture how gorgeous she probably looked now that she was a little older.

"Ass phat as fuck, too! Ain't no niggas around here can say they hit. She be fucking with a lame ass nigga from out there in Auburn Hills," Juice told him.

"You gone get me in real trouble with my girl," Steve said as he shook his head.

"Bro, your girl . . . You can do better than that. She be out here on bullshit with Esha, Candy and them. If you get Aaliyah, she gone be sick to her stomach. I'm telling you."

"See, that's why I can't ever call her. We just got back on a good track."

"Alright, so you ain't gone call her?"

"I will, eventually. I'll call her to see how she doing."

"I mean just be cool with her. She cool people. She don't be gossiping or nothing. She a good girl, bro. Trust me."

"Alright, alright. I'll holla at her."

CHAPTER
FIFTEEN

teve left, and texted the business phone, 'Ready.' A text came right back saying tomorrow, same time, same place. *Oh shit*, he thought to himself. He didn't think he would be able to get it that fast. He went home and Angelia was gone. He sat down on the couch to scroll through his phone and check his notifications for a few minutes with his bag sitting beside him. He thought for a few moments about what he needed to do. *Well, it's back to work*, he thought to himself as he stood up, grabbed the bag, and went to the bedroom upstairs. He counted up his money, put $15,000 aside for his uncle, and $450,000 to the side for Karo. He knew it was time to get a safe, so he left and drove up to a specialty store that sold them. After looking at his options, he selected one that he had delivered to a storage unit he had his mom get him and another one to be delivered to his house. The safes cost him $8,000 each. Both were 5 ft. 5 in. tall and pretty wide.

His mom didn't question why he needed a safe in a storage unit in her name. She just did as she was told. Plus, he gave her $10,000 to put toward her new place that was almost paid off. He needed to talk to his uncle. Everything was happening so fast. Steve was starting to get anxiety, so he drove up to see him. On the way there, Steve called James to let him know to find him a nice house. He didn't want all the drugs and money at his house. It was making him not be able to sleep, which was causing him to get paranoid.

Steve met his uncle in the same visitation room as last time at the federal prison in Milan. Everything looked gray now that it had been remodeled. The paint on the walls, the tile on the floor, the ceiling. It looked different from the last time he remembered. The only things that gave off any color were the vending machines. As always, his uncle was happy to see him and they greeted each other with a hug.

"I see they remodeled in here." Steve looked around.

"Yea, it's the Feds. If they need money, they can just print it," Swift joked.

"So, now I know your ass loaded. Filthy Rich!" Steve said while peering into Swift's eyes.

Swift laughed. "Why you say that, nephew?"

"Because this shit coming at a good price so I know you had to be doing your thing when you was out there. All them rumors I used to hear about you hauling millions . . . now I can see how."

Swift laughed again, "Maybe some rumors are true, but not all, nephew. So you doing well then, I'm guessing?"

"Yes, very well. She gave me 15 kilos. I just got them and I'm already cashing them out. This shit kinda scary how easy it is having a real plug. It's an easy sell. Can't nobody beat my price or quality. It's not even close, Unk."

Swift laughed. "That's how it should be nephew. Get a product that sells itself at a price nobody can beat and all that's left to do is count up the money coming in."

"Thank you, Unk. I really appreciate you doing this for sure."

"No problem, nephew. I knew you could handle this. This is why I chose you. You know I know people all over the place, plus I have plenty of partners I used to run with and I would never turn them on to Karo. Ever."

"Damn," Steve replied.

"So you paid off the 15. She about to load you up probably. That 15 was a test," Swift said as he looked at Steve.

"I can't even imagine."

"But listen, nephew. You have to start cleaning up the money you making. Start you a business, ASAP. Have you talked to CeCe about your credit?" Swift asked.

"I haven't even had the time, to be honest. I have to call her. I'll get on that," Steve replied, knowing he had a lot of shit to remember to do.

"Yea, don't neglect that. Your credit is a must. You have to learn how to play that game, I'm telling you. That way you don't have to cut corners to make shit happen. Get your girl, your mom, and your credit together."

"What's the point of credit though? I mean, like how it work?"

CHAPTER
SIXTEEN

redit is basically your creditability, but in the bank's eyes. For example, Karo gave you 15 kilos, you paid her, so she probably give you 50 now, etc. etc. So, same as the bank. They give you $5,000, you pay it back, then they gone offer to give you more. And you just keep building and building until you start playing with millions of dollars of the bank's money."

"I'ma get with CeCe soon."

"Yea, Lily got all kind of real estate, residential and commercial. That lady a millionaire, been a millionaire. You know most of that shit was mine. I been putting shit in her name for years, building her credit in all. CeCe will show you how to build your business credit too, which you will need. You build that and go get you some shit and let it pay itself off. Cashing out don't help you. Banks want to see you making payments."

"The girl I was telling you about last time, with the dump trucks, has all her trucks paid off."

"That's good, but if you trying to build, don't pay nothing off. Let it go for a couple years that way the banks can make they money too, which they will appreciate and want to give you more."

"I get it," Steve said, nodding his head. He had heard stories of his uncle moving big money around, but he didn't know that Swift knew so much about legit business and personal credit.

"I'ma just say this, you can borrow a million dollars with good credit faster than you can earn a million dollars. Obviously, with a real plug, it's different, but you get what I'm saying. When you was working your job, you probably felt like you was never getting ahead."

"Hell yeah, that shit was crazy. I couldn't get ahead. Something was always coming up, so I was always playing catch up."

"You know why?" Swift asked him, widening his eyes as he awaited his nephew's response.

"Not making enough money?" Steve asked.

"No . . . All the money you was making was going to your bills, rent, utilities, food, entertainment, and whatever else."

"What was I supposed to do?"

"Sacrifice is always needed when you tryna level up. Me? I woulda cut all bills, lived with my mom, and saved all the money I made for a year, then made my move to invest in something that could make me some money. You see, nephew, there are only so many hours in a day, and there's only one Swift. You gotta get your money to make money for you. Passive income."

"I feel you . . . Are you hungry?" Steve asked.

"Yea, grab me a few burgers and a Coke," Swift said. Steve walked up to the machines, got the burgers and Coke, microwaved the burgers, then came back with the food and all kinds of condiments to go with it.

"Thanks, nephew," Swift said, as he twisted the top off the 20 oz. bottle of Coke.

"You welcome. I was thinking, Unk . . . I think I should ask my girl to marry me."

Swift narrowed his eyes and leaned forward. He scooted his chair a little closer to Steve, and lowered his voice. "Nephew, I think you are a smart and intelligent young man, just not on the subject of women. Why on earth would you ask her to marry you after what just happened? It ain't even been a month yet. You gotta think, nephew," Swift said, shaking his head as he took a bite out of his burger.

"I feel like our bond is getting stronger. She told me how sorry she was, plus showed me that she got my back. Everything been back good with us. It's like that never happened. I cheated and she cheated, so we basically even," Steve said as he shrugged his shoulders.

Swift shook his head again. "No, nephew, that's not the way that goes." Swift was confused about why Steve loved her so much. "I just think it's too early, nephew. Give it some time before you do anything major like that."

"It's been seven years. She was with me when I was broke and now that I'm getting all this money, I think . . . I feel like this what she been waiting for me to do. She just wanted the best for both of us. I don't even care about the money, Unk. I care about being with who I love, having kids and a family. That's how she is as well. She Mexican. You know they huge on family. I had her get the birth control in her arm years ago. I think I should have her take it out," Steve said as he scratched his chin.

As bad as Swift wanted to tell him that he didn't think she was the one, he saw and heard how much his nephew loved this girl and didn't want to get on his bad side by trying to convince him why he shouldn't. He knew Steve had a lot to learn about women, and he was just going to let it play out. He didn't want to see Steve hurt in the meantime, so he decided to hold his tongue on the subject, for now.

CHAPTER
SEVENTEEN

When Steve left and finally got back to his phone, James had both texted and called, so he called him back.

"What up, bro?"

"Nothing. Leaving from up here with my uncle."

"Oh, ok. I'm at this crib. It's in Waterford. It's nice. I'ma send you the address for you to come see it. Shit, you might want to move here and make the other house . . . you know," James said.

Steve laughed as he put his hand on his forehead to keep the sun out of of his eyes. "Naw, I'ma stay where I'm at."

"Well, don't show Ang this house, because she gone want to move in this muthafucka," James told him.

Steve laughed. "Damn, it's like that?"

"Hell yeah! It's gone cost about $1,700 a month."

"Ok, that's cool. Tell him I want it. This another one of your uncle cribs?"

"Yep," James replied.

"Ok, bet. Grab it if you got the money. I'll give it back in a second. I'm heading that way now," Steve said as he tried to picture the house in his mind.

"Ok. I got you," James said and hung up the phone.

About an hour later, Steve pulled into the subdivision and he liked what he saw. He saw basketball hoops in driveways, kids playing in the front yards, and people walking their dogs. The subdivision wasn't flashy by any means. It looked safe and low key, which was exactly what he was wanting. As Steve pulled up, he already knew that this house would work for his needs. Once Steve walked in the door, he signed the lease for a year without any hesitation. The house was very nice and much bigger than the one he lived in. From what he had seen while driving in, the neighborhood looked much better, too. It was absolutely perfect to Steve. This is where he wanted to keep everything. Nobody would know about this spot except for him and James, who he trusted with his life. The spot was out of the way, so nobody he knew would ever see him coming and going. Now all he needed was to get some furniture in the house to make it look like somebody was actually living there. The garage was attached to the house so he could drive straight in and out, without anyone seeing him. Steve was going to hire a landscaping company to keep the grass cut, and put in a few new shrubs and flowering plants so the home looked well maintained like the others in the subdivision. Steve asked James if he could research a company in the area for him. Of course, James took care of it for him, and had a company contracted for the work the same day.

Steve noticed his phone ringing from a number he had never seen before. "Hello," he answered.

"Hey! How are you?"

"I'm good. Who is this?" Steve replied to the unknown caller.

"This is Aaliyah." Steve immediately had a big smile on his face. "Juice told me to call you," Aaliyah continued. "He mentioned you was interested in the real estate market. I help him find a lot of the houses he buys, probably all of them, so I wanted to help you as well."

"Oh, ok, ok. How you been? I appreciate you calling. I haven't seen you in forever. I thought you moved away or something."

She giggled. "Well, I did, to New Jersey with my boyfriend. He played college ball out there but got injured. That brought us back to Michigan a few years ago, and I just been staying out the way. I don't deal with too many outside of my family."

"Dang, sorry about that injury. I'm so surprised right now to hear from you."

"Aw, whatever. We should link up sometime and catch up."

"Yea, for sure. When? I mean, let's do that soon."

"Well, Juice and them going to have a little something at their house on Saturday. If you want to stop by, I'll be there."

"I'm not even gone lie to you," Steve began, "I don't be doing stuff like that."

"Too many people? Ok, let's just do brunch sometime soon. I have your number and you have mine. Call me anytime."

"Ok, I will for sure. Talk to you soon."

CHAPTER
EIGHTEEN

e hung up and was sweating. He was so excited to be in contact with her. He couldn't wait to see how good she was looking these days. As soon as he hung up with her, he called the twins and told them he was on his way to see them. He went home and grabbed two kilos and stashed them. Shila was texting him the whole way there. She was sending pics, and Steve could tell she was tipsy.

Shila: I miss you so much!

Steve: Miss you too.

Shila: I want to be your girlfriend.

Steve: I know boo.

Shila: What I gotta do? I like how you move. You not like these dudes out here.

Steve: Just be you, like you doing. What's different about me?

Shila: These niggas out here want more attention than the females. You not like that.

Steve: LOL yea I be chillin.

Shila: I know. I like that.

Steve: We going to do something with trucks soon.

Shila: I hope so. I'm excited.

Steve: For real, I need to be part of that.

Shila: You got it baby. Whatever you want and need me to do.

Steve: I appreciate you.

Shila: No problem. I told you I got you. You my baby. I see your rat ass girlfriend here.

Steve: LOL Chillout.

Shila: You deserve so much better than her. She a sack chaser.

Steve: Why don't you like her?

Shila: Because I just don't. It's a lot of reasons. When can I see you?

Steve: We gone link soon. How long you gone be up there?

Shila: Until you tell me to leave.

Steve: LOL you silly.

Shila: I'm serious.

Steve: I'm not going to tell you to leave if you not ready to. Enjoy yourself, ain't you with your homegirls?

Shila: Yea we all here, but I rather be with you.

Steve: You making me blush.

Shila: I'll make you cum too.

Steve: Oouu shit.

Shila: In my mouth.

Steve: Sure will.

Shila: I want you right now. Where you at?

Steve: LOL taking care of some business right now boo.

Shila: Ok, I'll let you continue. I'll text you later.

Steve: Ok.

Soon, Steve was pulling up on the twins. They were surprised everything checked out for the price they were paying. They paid for one and he fronted them another one. The twins were more than happy to keep this situation rolling as long as they could. Steve told them just to call him when they were done. It was a quick meeting with them, because Steve had more stops to make. After leaving, he stopped in Redford to pull up on a guy he knew from way back in the day named Kane. Steve got off I-96 West at Telegraph, smelling the White Castle on the corner before arriving at the twins house.

"What up, doe? Kane said, always happy to see Steve.

"Chillin, man. What you got going on out here?" Steve said, stepping out the car.

"Same ol', same ol', fucking with that white girl."

Kane was a good looking young man in his late 20's with caramel skin covered in many, yet tasteful, tattoos. He had perfectly done, tight braids complemented by a thin mustache and goatee. He was wearing a red and black Gucci outfit, with the shoes to match. He always smelled strong like fresh weed and expensive cologne.

"How much you paying right now?" Steve asked.

"I'm getting a half of a brick for $24,000. Shit high right now."

"Is it that shit though?"

"Yea, it's good. It be off and on though. I really need a new plug on it. You can get it?"

"Yea, probably better too. Bout $22,500."

"Man, if you can do that, that would be love. When can I check it out?"

"Follow me to the Yak. I'll give you a piece."

Kane laughed. "I forgot all y'all in Pontiac call it Yaktown. I ain't heard that in a while. Ok, I'll meet you out there. I'ma go to the Coney Island out there on Perry, across from that gas station. You know I gotta grab that every time I come to the Yak."

Steve laughed. "Ok, bet. I'll see you up there in a sec."

CHAPTER
NINETEEN

Jon Jon and Angelia had been at the day party for several hours and he was ready to go, but Angelia wanted to stay with Esha, Candy, and the rest of her girls. Jon Jon saw all the guys there eyeing her, since she was definitely one of the finest chicks in there. She had got her face made up flawless, and she was Chanel'd down, in all white. She had on white high heeled shoes with her toes done in a deep aqua blue. Her ass was busting through the thin white pants she was wearing and everybody there was checking her out. She looked good; nobody could deny that. Although he didn't want to leave her there, Jon Jon left anyway. He had been sitting by her the whole time, and his baby momma was noticeably pissed about it, but she kept her cool and didn't say anything. After Jon Jon left, the girls came by to tease Angelia for a minute.

"Bout damn time. He was cuffing your ass," Esha said while taking a drink of her wine.

Angelia giggled. "You silly. That's my baby. He was just trying to show me off," Angelia said as she waved her hands down from her chest down her legs, emphasizing that she knew she looked good in her outfit.

"Whatever. It's millionaires in here. Kamozy been trying to get to your ass for hours. You need to go talk to him and gone ahead and introduce me to the friend," Esha said, high fiving Candy while winking at Angelia.

"Me too, shit!" Candy added.

"What did he say?" Angelia asked curiously.

"He just said, tell your homegirl to get at me, and he gave his number," Esha said, giving her the paper.

Angelia got the paper and sent him a selfie. He responded right away telling her and her girls to come upstairs to VIP. "He said come to VIP," Angelia said.

"Shut up! Let's go!" Esha shouted, getting up and wasting no time.

On the way to VIP, Angelia ran into Ace, a guy she saw every now and then, but it had been months since she saw him last. Ace had always been in pretty good shape, but he looked like he had put on at least a good 10 pounds of more muscle.

"Dang, you just cut me off?" she said, giving him a hug.

"Naw, I just got out a few days ago. I had to do 45 days for a violation, and I lost your number. I hit you up on your Instagram. You ain't open it though," Ace said with a look on his face that put the blame back on her.

"I be having so much mail on there. Here, take my number," she said as she grabbed his phone out of his hands and saved her number in it.

"You still with ol' dude?" Ace asked while looking her up and down, noticing, like everyone else at the party did, that Angelia looked like a model.

"Yea, but I can get away," she said, winking at him and walking up the stairs to VIP. Ace was a known dealer around Pontiac and

Detroit. He was doing well for himself and all the girls in the city were crazy about him. He was always dressed well and drove nice cars. Ace was 30 years old with medium brown skin, and looked like he could be Usher's brother. He kept a low bald fade with a thin lined beard and mustache. Angelia was happy to see him, and glad to be back in contact with him again.

CHAPTER
TWENTY

As the girls continued to make their way up the stairs, Kamozy was waiting at the top, and gave all the girls hugs. They could see a beautiful VIP area with an all glass wall with a sliding door at the back overlooking the swimming pool. Several small bars were set up both inside and outside staffed with female bartenders dressed in black polo shirts with short white skirts and black high heels. A few large, tropical plants adorned the outer corners of the glass wall. The sound of glasses clinking, giggling, bottles of champagne popping, and music could be heard in the background. People were sitting in white leather chairs and standing around in circles around white high top bar style tables with chrome legs. After greeting them, Kamozy turned around, walked back into the party, and introduced the girls to several of his homies. After everyone seemed to be comfortable, he reached out his arm, taking Angelia by the hand, and leading her to a white leather sofa in the corner where it wasn't as loud.

"Have a seat. What you drinking, beautiful?" he asked, looking closely into her eyes. He knew how to impress chicks with little glances and small acts of kindness.

"Margarita," Angelia replied as she looked down at her almost empty glass, giving it a tilt to the side.

"Grab a margarita for me, please," he said to the waitress who nodded, smiled, and walked away.

"Thank you," she said, smiling while making herself more comfortable.

"You welcome. What's up with you? I ain't never seen you in here before. You know I'm the king of the city, so why I don't know you?" he asked as he scooted himself a little closer.

She giggled. "I don't be out much. I'm Angelia," she said as she extended her hand.

"I give hugs, baby, not handshakes," he told her as he reached his arms out. She giggled and gave him a hug. "Damn, you wearing my favorite perfume. That's Chanel?" Kamozy asked as he took a sip of his drink.

The waitress brought over Angelia's margarita and handed it to her.

"Thank you," Angelia said. "Yes, Kamozy, it's Chanel. It's my favorite perfume too." She looked down at her green margarita, then she took a sip. "This is good!"

"Yea, they make the margarita's with Patron. People here be loving them that way. So was that your man you was with all day earlier?"

She giggled. "No, just a friend."

"You too fine for him. You need to be fucking with a nigga like me. I'll have you right by my side while we flying all over the world. Whatever you wanted, you'd be having if you was my girl."

"Oh, yeah?" Angelia smiled. Maybe the alcohol had a little to do with it, but she was really starting to feel him.

"Hell yea. I'll spoil you. You should do this photo shoot with me this weekend. I'll pay you $1,500, too. It's for my album cover."

"I'm cool with that," Angelia said casually, trying to hide her excitement.

"What y'all doing after this? I got a mansion party later, invites only. It's only gone be like 50 people total. Got a pool and everything. We should roll there together. You can ride with me in the back of the Maybach. We been drinking, so we can't be out here driving and shit. I'll make sure your girls get there too," he said smoothly. His offer was hard for her to resist, and the liquor had Angelia ready to go anywhere with him, even if a Maybach and a mansion weren't involved.

"Ok, that sounds good," Angelia replied. She never imagined dating a rapper before, but Kamozy was cool. She liked his swag. He was tall, about 6 ft. 3 in., nicely built, with perfectly lined up facial hairs, a thin beard, and caramel skin with straight, white, pretty teeth. He wore a big gold chain with a diamond charm that spelled his name and a bust down Presidential Rolex. Kamozy was the hottest rapper in Michigan at the moment, and Angelia wanted to know all about him. She always heard people talking about him and listening to his music and now, here she was, sitting next to him, being invited to cruise in his Maybach to a mansion party. She was in a mild state of disbelief, but she was having a good time. As it got later, they continued to talk and drink. He told her a lot about himself, and she did the same. They were the same horoscope sign, and they were getting along great.

CHAPTER
TWENTY-ONE

"Y ou know, you real cool. I'm glad I met you."
"Same here."

"I'm not sure if you gone be able to handle my freaky side though," Angelia said with a matter-of-fact look on her face. She scooted a little closer to him, and put her hand on his leg.

He laughed. "Why you think that? What you one of them weird ass chicks that like to be dressed up in leather, wearing masks, and getting beat?"

She giggled. "Nooo! Well, I do like rough, shit-talking sex. Like throw me wherever and smack me, spit on me type stuff, definitely smack my ass."

"Oh, we perfect. I like all that. I didn't know that was freaky. I just thought that was normal."

They both laughed, and he leaned his shoulder into her playfully.

"You might can't handle me though."

"Why is that?"

"Not many chicks can handle this," he said, grabbing his dick through his pants.

"You have a big dick?"

"I do."

"How big?" she asked as her eyes widened a little.

"Bout 12 inches," he replied casually while letting go of his dick.

"Damn. Yea I don't know about that. You will kill me."

They laughed.

"No, I won't. I know what I'm doing with this. I ain't gone kill you. I might kill that pussy though for sure. She gone be fucked up," he said joking and laughing.

"I'll have to see it, you know, see how fat it is and all that," she told him.

"Come on, let me show you." He stood up and grabbed her hand. She put her drink down and followed him to a bathroom. He opened the door for her, locked it behind him, wasted no time pulling his pants down, and leaning back against the black marble sink. His dick was slightly hard from the conversation. He folded his arms and looked down at Angelia, giving her a minute to respond.

"Yea, that's big. I'd give it a try though," she said lifting it up. "Heavy dick."

He laughed. "You think you can handle that?"

"Honestly, I don't know. Nothing this big ever been in me."

"You might as well suck it and get familiar with it."

She looked up at him. She liked him and was tempted, but wasn't quite sure about sucking his dick. "You silly, boy. I'm not about to suck your dick. I bet you be getting all the girls like that, huh?

He laughed. "What you mean? Like what?"

"The groupie chicks. They just be sucking your dick and you be on to the next?"

"Naw, naw, naw," he said, pulling up his pants.

CHAPTER
TWENTY-TWO

Steve was chilling at home in the bed texting Angelia. She had told him that she wouldn't be home until later. He told her to be careful and that he was going to go ahead and go to sleep because he had to get up early. Shila wasn't invited to the mansion party, but she saw Angelia leave with Kamozy. Everyone did, and most of the girls were jealous because it wasn't them. Shila started texting Steve.

Shila: What you doing boo?

Steve: Laying in bed. What about you?

Shila: Driving home from the club. I wish I was laying next to you.

Steve: That sounds good don't it?

Shila: So good. It's only 9, why you in bed already?

Steve: I'm reading, laying down, by the time I get done, I will be knocked out.

Shila: What you reading?

Steve: The Millionaire Next Door.

Shila: Is it good? Sounds good.

Steve: Yea it's real good.

Shila: I didn't know you read.

Steve: LOL what that suppose to mean?

Shila: Niggas don't read so I'm surprised you read.

Steve: Ohh, hell yea I read. My uncle told me, all the game is in the books.

Shila: That's a fact.

Steve: What you about to do?

Shila: I was trying to see you but I see you in for the night.

Steve: Soon we will link.

Shila: You always say that and don't be coming through.

Steve: I have a girlfriend, I be tryna be a good dude.

Shila: Too good of a dude. You must don't know your girl.

Steve: Why you keep throwing shots and not telling me what you mean?

Shila: I'm just saying, your girl at the club twerking, and you at home reading a book.

Steve: Twerking? You silly LOL

Shila: Lol

It was around 3:30am that night when Angelia was driving home tipsy. She was definitely feeling the alcohol, but she was driving alright for the most part. As she got off the freeway, a cop car pulled out of the gas station behind her and started to follow her. Angelia glanced in her rearview mirror. The cop car was right up behind her, and she could see him glancing at his computer, running her plates. *Damn*, she thought to herself. Her heart started pounding. If he pulled her over at this hour, he would definitely breathalyze her, and she'd fail. Her hands started sweating as she sat up a little straighter, trying to focus on driving perfectly. "He ain't leaving," Angelia said to herself as she glanced one more time in her rearview. She saw the blue and red lights flip on, heard the siren chirp, and her heart dropped. She then heard the roar of an engine, as the cop car raced by her driver's side with his lights and sirens on, clearly heading to someone else. Esha was about a half mile behind her and called her. She saw the cop car, and was worried for Angelia.

"What, Esha?"

Esha giggled. "You alright? I saw that cop car."

"Yea, I was scared as hell. I thought he was gone pull me over for sure."

"You mad at me?"

"No, I'm just tired."

"Oh, did y'all do it?" Esha asked.

"No, he was trying but I wasn't about to fuck him that fast. I did let him eat me out though."

"He ate you out?" Esha asked, shocked.

"Did he? Ate the ass and all. He kept wanting to eat my pussy, but I came twice. I was straight."

"Damn, bitch! You my bitch! You made Kamozy eat your pussy! He be talking all that shit in his raps like he don't be eating pussy and ate the soul out you."

They both laughed.

"You got some dick?"

"You already know I did. Candy was fucking too," she said, laughing.

"What about Kim?"

"I think she gave the dude head. She was on her cycle. We had fun tonight, girl. There was some real ballers up in there."

"Yea, there were. I had fun too. Well, I'm bout to sneak in this house in a second. Kamozy calling me. I'll call you tomorrow."

"Ok, drive safe."

CHAPTER
TWENTY-THREE

"Hello," Angelia answered.

"Hey, just making sure you made it home safely."

"Yea, I'm about to pull up in a second. I had to pick up my car. I'm so tired. You wore me out."

He laughed. "You didn't know I could salsa like that, huh?"

"I sure didn't. Most black men can't salsa, so yes I was surprised."

"I didn't' want your sexy ass to leave. I hope I get to see you again soon soon, before the photo shoot if you can."

"We will see. I had fun, Kamozy. Thank you."

"You welcome. No problem. Goodnight."

"Goodnight, hun."

When she walked in the house, she set her car keys and purse down on the kitchen counter. She poured herself a glass of water, downed it, and went to the bedroom. Steve was asleep and snoring. She got undressed, taking everything off except her panties. She threw one of Steve's t-shirts on, pulled back the covers, crawled in bed next to him and went right to sleep.

Steve was up and out of the house early the following morning. It was about 7:30 AM as he pulled into the gas station to fill up. While he was filling his tank, a fat, bald white guy covered in tattoos with a long beard pulled up on an all black and chrome Harley with loud pipes. Steve was admiring how clean the dude's bike looked as the morning sun reflected off the black and chrome.

"Nice bike," Steve said to the dude.

The guy thanked him, and Steve drove off. *I gotta get me a Harley one day,* he thought. He was waiting outside his mom's place when a Mexican drove up with a longer truck this time that had two cars on it. He took one off and gave Steve the paperwork. It was a white Kia Cadenza with a black leather interior. Steve actually liked the car for himself. He signed everything and gave the guy the duffle bag full of money. As the guy left, Steve received a text message that read, 'Middle arm console.' He opened the door and got the paper out of the middle console and began reading. This stash spot was a little more complicated than the last one, so he just drove to the new house, pulled into the garage, and parked.

To get to his spot, he had to take out the back seat of the car after turning the car off, putting the car in neutral, turning the steering wheel all the way to the right, holding it, while pumping the breaks 4 times, then the gas pedal 6 times until he heard a noise that sounded like something was being unlocked. When he heard the noise, he opened the back door. There was a piece raised up like the hood on a car and there was a combination he had to put in to open the metal covering. He put the code from the paper into the lock, and it opened, revealing a large compartment filled with kilos. He counted each kilo as he pulled them out, one by one. "46, 47, 48, 49, 50, 51, 52, 53, 54, 55, 56, 57, 58, 59, 60. Damn," he said to himself. He carried all of them inside and stashed 40 of them in the attic that could be accessed from the bedroom closet. He left the other 20 out to work on. He then had James come get him and drop him back off at his mom's to get his car.

"Was that your new car, baby? That was nice," his mom said.

"Yea, thank you. You need anything? I'm getting ready to go to work."

"Nope. I'm good baby. I'll call you later. Be safe. Love you."

"Love you too."

CHAPTER
TWENTY-FOUR

Steve and James had been out all morning ripping and running around, grabbing stuff to get the new place in order. They had to bring all the utensils over to the crib. They stopped by Home Depot for some of the basic stuff they needed like Rubbermaid trash cans and garbage bags, buckets, cleaning supplies, and a few other things. Then they ran to a popular furniture store to supply the whole house. He bought a California King for the master bedroom along with two nightstands and a dresser. He picked out a twin bed for the second bedroom, a nightstand, and a computer desk. For the third bedroom, where the real work would take place, they bought 2 long tables and 2 folding chairs. All the furniture was getting delivered the following day, and James made plans to be there for the delivery. They drove back to the house, and dropped off the supplies.

By the time they brought everything in the house, it was 5 PM and Angela had called Steve home because she had made dinner. She made ribeye steak, baked potatoes, and green beans which was one of his favorite meals. When he opened the door of the house, the smell of the food hit him right in the face.

"Thank you, baby. You didn't need to make me nothing," he said as he walked up to her and kissed her. "The food smells good as hell."

"You welcome, sweetie."

"I been missing your ass. Ever since I got you that car, you been out on me."

She giggled. "That's not true. I know you been busy doing what you doing, and I been trying to get myself out there as well. I got booked by Kamozy for a photo shoot on Saturday, $1,500."

"Oh, damn, that's dope. Congrats on that. I mean, I ain't surprised with you walking around looking as beautiful as you do all the time."

"I know, right? I'm so excited!"

"You gotta get some nice shit to wear. He doing big things out here."

"He's paying for everything. I don't have to buy anything."

"Oh, wow, look at you. You go, baby."

She smiled. "Thanks, boo."

"This shit is so, so good." Steve was licking his fingers and chewing.

She giggled. "Slow down," she joked.

"What your daddy say about them bricks he had got?"

"Oh, he loved them. He said he is going to buy more soon."

"That's what's up. I have to drive out to Saginaw today. You want to ride with me?"

"I suppose to link up with Esha in a couple hours, boo. I wish you woulda told me earlier."

"No biggie, I'm just going there and coming right back."

"You going to see Free?"

"Yea, taking him something out there."

"Tell him I said hello."

Free was a good friend of Angelia and Steve and had been around them since before they were even together. He was a hustler, as well as a goon, but was like family to them. Steve was excited to get out there to catch up with him.

CHAPTER
TWENTY-FIVE

He soon started picking his plate up and bringing it over to the sink. He grabbed the pan off the oven, and Angelia stopped him. "Not today, baby. I'm cleaning up," she said, turning on the sink.

After she finished the dishes, Steve saw a video call coming through on his phone. It was CeCe.

"What's up, lady," he answered.

"Hey, how are you? Is this a good time for you?"

"Yea, yea, this good. My girl right here too, so it's perfect. This way she can hear what you saying as well. I want to get her in position for a mortgage."

"Ok, sounds good."

"Hey, baby, come meet my cousin in Alabama. This my uncle's daughter CeCe."

"Hey, how you doing? I'm Angelia," she said, moving her chair next to Steve and waving.

"This the one I was telling you about that can fix credit and stuff."

"Oh, ok, ok. Yes, I'm ready to hear what I need to do."

"Hold on, CeCe. Let me grab a pen and some paper." He got up and went and got a notebook and came back, using the pen that sat on the table. He set the phone up that way CeCe could see them both. CeCe looked like she was in an office. There were nice shelves behind her with what looked like real estate and investment books on them along with a few pictures.

"Ok, let me first start off by saying, credit is a game. The key to winning is to learn the rules of the game. This credit stuff can be used as an asset or can be your biggest liability. Me personally, I only use credit to make more money."

"How you make money off credit?" Angelia asked. Steve wanted to answer that question, but he stayed silent and let CeCe respond.

"For example, let's say you have a 700 credit score with a good history, and you want to make money . . . well, never mind that. Let's just say you have like a Macy's credit card, a Victoria's Secret credit card, and a Home Depot credit card. Which one you think is more valuable?"

"Victoria's Secret?" Angelia guessed and Steve and CeCe laughed.

"Well . . . I shoulda said that different."

"Oh, you selling pussy now?" Steve joked.

They all laughed.

"No," she said as she playfully smacked his arm.

"Ok, so I'm in real estate, so I buy houses and fix them up to rent and sometimes sell. So, a Home Depot card would be way more valuable to me because I can buy paint, bathroom stuff, carpet, anything inside the house, you know."

"Oh, ok. I see what you saying. You can use your regular credit cards for that as well, like Visa, Mastercard, and all that, right?" Angelia asked.

"Yes," CeCe answered.

"I get it, girl. Basically, don't be using your credit cards to go buy clothes and shoes and stuff. Use it on stuff that's gone make you money?"

"Yep."

"Well, I failed that! All my credit cards was spent on BS, girl."

They laughed.

"No worries, that's why I'm here, to help you clean all that bad stuff up and get you back on the road to success. I know how bad credit can make you feel, especially when you unsure what to do and how to do it."

Angelia and Steve both agreed with head nods.

CHAPTER
TWENTY-SIX

"So, my rule is, if you want to buy yourself something nice on your credit card, if you can't pay for it, or aren't going to be able to pay for it in full in 30 days, don't swipe it."

"I'ma write that down," Angelia said. "I like that rule."

"Our parents should have told us about how to use credit and what to use it for, but, honestly, they had no idea themselves what to do with credit. Nobody taught them and when they was coming up, they didn't have the internet to go search this info like we do. I remember my mom used to be like, 'Stay away from credit cards. It's bad,' but I always wondered why she was saying that because the white people I was going to school with all had credit cards and nice cars, but my mom at the time didn't have anything so I was confused. I started googling stuff, reading books, going to seminars, and all kinds of stuff learning about credit. And once I found out people can use credit to get rich, I went to my mom and started wrestling with her mentality, trying to give her a new mindset about credit. It was hard, but she wound up understanding it. Plus, Swift was in her ear as well. She took it and ran with it, and now my mom making hella money. She don't use her money to do anything anymore. She goes straight to one of her lenders and banks to get the money."

"What if she has the money in her bank account she's asking for?"

"That's when they give you the money the fastest, when you don't need it."

"Oh, wow. That makes sense, I guess."

"Yes. So before I go on with that, have you guys pulled your credit reports lately?"

They both said no.

"Ok, I'm going to pull it now if that's ok with you."

"I usually look at Credit Karma for mine," Angelia said.

"That's not going to show you everything. You need to pull your actual credit report, that way you can see everything. You get one free one a year at annualcreditreport.com. That's what I use right now. What's your social, date of birth, and full name, Steve?"

Steve gave her all his info plus answered the security questions and Angelia did the same. "Ok, Steve. You have a 603, nothing in good standing, but you have 6 collections which I can get off. Also, you see where it says Steve Tristen Burden, Steve T. Burden, and Steve Burden?" She showed him on the screen.

"Yea, what that mean?"

"Also, it's 4 different addresses and 3 phone numbers. What that means is, when you went to apply for a credit card or whatever you was trying to get, you wrote your name different every time on the application, which they reported to the credit bureaus. That's what's showing up here. Not saying it's not your name, but most people don't know, having all this different info can effect your score by like 20-30 points. So the first thing you want to do is get all the personal info current, and you can do this by phone, fax, the quick way. On the phone it may take about 2 hours on hold, well, maybe not that long, but you know what I mean. So write this down, call Experian, TransUnion, and Equifax and change all your info to wherever you at now."

Steve wrote down the names of the bureaus CeCe told him to contact. "Do my id have to match also?"

"Good question. Yes, it should, so if y'all just moved, go get all that done. I make all my clients have this stuff updated right before I start disputing stuff. Also, after y'all get your license together, well Steve, because her situation may be different, but Angelia, you still need to do the personal info part for sure, no matter what your report look like. So, update that because your personal info not matching can cause you to get denied for something you really should get approved for. They have computer systems they run you through and if something is off, it's going to trip the system and you will get denied, so this is important."

"Dang, I never knew that. Why don't they teach us this in school? I feel like I been living under a rock and we just getting started," Angelia giggled.

"That's a good question. I don't know the answer to that one, but they need to start, but they probably won't. You know schools set you up to be a consumer and to get a job, so even if they did teach about credit, they probably would tell you to get credit cards and pay your bills on time, that's about it."

They all laughed.

"Seriously, it's crazy. That's why we have to take the initiative to educate ourselves and not count on schools or colleges . . . Also, before I get off track, when you guys call and update the info, they may ask why you want the old stuff deleted. Make sure you say, it's inaccurate information. Keep it simple. Since all the stuff you have on here is negative accounts, Steve, you want to delete all the addresses and give them your current one. If you had a positive account on here, I would tell you to keep that address on there. Also, if it's old jobs on your report, delete that too. I don't see a job on here though, so you good. Yours going to be easy. You want to do it the quick way or in a few months? Because I can dispute this stuff with letters through mail, but you going to have to be patient."

"Naw, I want it done ASAP," he said, laughing.

"Ok, we can do a police report . . . online," she said, giggling. "Relax, I see your eyes widen, when I mentioned the police."

"Right, I'm like, what," he said, laughing.

"Naw, it ain't like ya think. It's simple. You just go online, and fill out the questions they ask you. Michigan should have a site. I'll have to look it up, but you going to list all the negative accounts and tell them you're not responsible for this stuff. I can do that for you. All I'm going to do is fill out the report. Also, I'm going to attach affidavits to it as well which will make it an identity theft report. I'm going to send it to all three credit bureaus. From my experience, it's always been a piece of cake, so this will be simple. I've done thousands of these," she giggled. "But once it's cleaned you have to follow my instructions so I can build you up, so you can get anything you want."

CHAPTER
TWENTY-SEVEN

can see you know what you talking about. I ain't never heard any of this so I'ma listen to you for sure," Angelia said as she scribbled down a few more notes.

"Better yet, I'm going to still give you a plan. Write this down too, so after we get everything negative off there, you're going to call me and I'm going to add you to three of my mom's credit cards. This is kind of a major cheat code. She has a $40,000 credit limit."

"What you mean add me? How you do that?"

"It's called an Authorized User. Any time you have a major credit card, you usually have like 5 slots on there where you can add people to your card, and they send you a credit card with their name on it. In this case, I'll add you on three of hers, the cards will come to her. You don't get a card, nor do you use it. The way it will help you is, all her credit history from those cards will roll over to your credit profile, which will boost your credit score up over 100 points within weeks, or as soon as it reports."

"Damn."

"Yea, that's what the white people been doing for years. They just piggy back off each other. That's how they kids be having 750's when they turn 18. They add them when they were 16 or so."

"Oh wow, yea, my parents ain't know nothing about that. I didn't even have a credit score when I turned 18," Angelia said.

"Me either, girl, so Authorized Users is for sure a cheat code. They have companies that sell tradelines or Authorized User spaces. It be about $500 a slot depending on the limit and the age of the card. This free for y'all. I'm not going to charge you guys and you're getting 10 year old cards with $40,000 limits, so it's going to really impact your score quickly in a positive way."

"Where can I read about all this stuff at?" Angelia asked.

"There's plenty of books online. Just look for a high rated one. Go to Amazon and type in words like, build credit up, 700 credit score, 800 credit score. Just play with different word phrases and see what books pop up, then start reading, and you will learn so much stuff. It's going to piss you off that nobody ever told you this stuff."

They both giggled. "I'm already pissed off," Angelia said, giggling while shaking her head.

"I know what you mean, trust me," CeCe said. "And I haven't even got to the credit side of the game, where before you start disputing stuff, you need to freeze your reports on Lexus Nexus, Innovis, and Advanced Resolution Services."

"Wait, wait, see I see this ain't just A, B, C, D, so we going to have to pay for your services because we don't know nothing about all them names you just said," Angelia said.

They all laughed.

"I'm still stuck on what the hell is an affidavit," Steve said, laughing.

"All an affidavit is, is a statement wrote, confirmed by oath, like a sworn statement. And actually, that's how I dispute when I dispute. I don't always use dispute letters. I send they butts an affidavit. Once they see one of those, they know not to play," she said, giggling.

"So where that come from?"

"An affidavit?"

"Yea."

"You just make it. It just has to have 'Affidavit' at the top. It sounds fancy, but it's really just a letter with that word at the top. You get it notarized and have a witness sign it. It's that simple."

"See, ok, yea, how much you will charge us to just do everything?" Steve asked as he jokingly threw his hands up in the air.

CeCe giggled. "I thought you wanted to learn this stuff. Don't get scared. You know that whole give a man a fish vs. teach a man to fish thing. . . "

They laughed. "I'm not scared. It's just more stuff than I thought to it," he said.

"I still want to learn, CeCe I'ma just start reading books and calling you, but I still want you to clean mine up the fast way," Angelia told her.

"No problem. I'm not going to charge y'all, and get my number from Steve and call me anytime."

"I will, for sure."

"I'm still shooting you some money for your help."

"Nope. I'm not accepting," she said.

They all laughed.

"Whatever, CeCe. Ok, you can do both of ours and let us know what we need to do when it's time to build," he said.

"So, y'all don't want to know that before you start disputing, you want to go to optoutprescreen.com and opt out . . ."

"Bye, CeCe!" Steve said, laughing. "Thank you though, for real."

"Yes, thank you, CeCe. Nice to meet you."

CeCe giggled, as she was just messing around with them. She truly loved what she did, and she knew a lot about the subject. She was always learning more, and loved sharing what she knew with others. "Ok, ok, I quit," CeCe said with a smile. "Nice to meet you too, Angelia. I'll talk to y'all soon. Bye," she said as she waved.

CHAPTER
TWENTY-EIGHT

Steve hung up. "That was more than I expected," he said.

Angelia giggled. "Yes, I agree, but at least we in good hands. I feel like she's going to get us all the way together. She's smart!"

"Yea, she will. My uncle told me she was really good at what she did."

"I'm excited. Ok, I gotta go shower and get ready."

"Ok," Steve replied as he gathered up the few pages of notes he had taken and set them in a neat pile.

As Angelia was going up the stairs, she felt her phone vibrate in her pocket. She took out her phone and saw a text from Jon Jon, asking her to borrow 10 dollars. She knew what he meant. They had already talked about what he would be asking, and where they would meet. She turned around, walked back downstairs and found Steve in the kitchen getting himself a drink out of the fridge.

"What's up, baby? I thought you was getting in the shower?"

"Baby, my dad said he wants another 10 kilos. Can you get that?"

"Yea, I can go grab it right now."

"Ok, I'ma jump in the shower. I'll take them to him when you come back."

"Alright, I need to get you a stash spot in your car. I don't want you to be riding with all that. I can get it done in the morning if you gone be here."

"Yea, tomorrow is cool."

"Ok, I'll be back in a little bit."

"I forgot to tell you, Candy is getting put out of her house. She asked me to stay here for a little while, until she gets her stuff together."

"Wasn't she just at the day party with you?"

"Yea . . . what that gotta do with anything?" Angelia said as she gave Steve a glare.

"Why she partying and she broke?"

"People be having to get out, Steve, when they stressed out."

"Fuck all that. Get out for what? You need to be finding a job. Why you ain't help her out? Don't you got money?"

"Well, I spent it . . . But Candy-."

"You getting $10,000 off this play you about to make. You can help her."

Angelia rolled her eyes. "I'm trying to get myself together. She can't just stay over for a little while? That girl spends her money on stupid stuff. She need to sell some of those Louie purses."

"I see you got 3 Chanel purses. Those aren't cheap neither. You probably need to be making better decisions with your money as well."

She rolled her eyes. "Whatever, Steve. she's going to be staying for a little while. She will be here later," she said as she continued up the stairs, not turning around to look at him.

Steve didn't have anything against Candy. As a matter of fact, he found Candy to be pretty funny even though he generally didn't like being around Angelia's friends. He was confused, though, as to why Angelia didn't want to help her. He noticed that Angelia was acting different. Something was up. He didn't know if it was the money she was now making, the Chanel purses and outfits she was wearing, or what. He hoped she wasn't silently in competition with Candy. Candy had been around since they got together, and although Candy always had more money than Angelia, it never seemed to be a problem before. Now, though, the tables were turning, and Angelia didn't want to give her any money. Steve didn't understand why. He shook his head about why he was even spending his energy thinking about the situation, but he couldn't help it. He really cared for Angelia, and wanted to make sure she wasn't heading down the wrong path. A text came through.

Shila: Baby, where you at?

Steve: In route to handle something real quick.

Shila: Stop by real quick. It'll be fast.

CHAPTER
TWENTY-NINE

S teve wondered what was so important. Although she wasn't on the way to where he was going, she wasn't far out of the way, so he decided he would go there. When he got there about 15 minutes later, he parked his car in the garage. Shila opened up the door looking sexy. Steve got out of the car, and walked into the house.

"What's up?" he asked, following behind her, watching the way the purple shorts climbed in her butt.

"I missed you. Sit down," she said, pushing him down on the couch, and getting on her knees. "It's gone be fast, relax," she said, pulling his pants down. In his mind he thought she had something important to tell him, but instead now he had to prepare himself for what she was about to do. It didn't take long before his dick was standing at attention. She knew what she was doing. She stroked and sucked his dick consistently as she massaged his balls with her hand. It felt so good to him as she did her thing. He realized in that moment how much he missed her head. It wasn't long before his dick was erupting like a volcano, and she slurped every drop of his cum up, including the cum that ran down his shaft to his balls.

"Shit, baby. Fuck," he whispered as he watched her clean him up with her mouth and swallowed it all. She then left and came back with a warm towel. "God damn." He shook his head speechless. His legs felt weak.

"Ok, go handle your business. I'll text you later," she told him as she held her hand out to help him up from the couch and walked him back to the door.

"Ok, cool, I -," he was talking, but she shut the door.

"Bye, boo."

He smiled to himself. He loved the feeling that was taking over him at the moment. She didn't waste anytime with him, and didn't even take a minute for unnecessary small talk. Shila knew he was busy, so she took care of business and sent him on his way. Steve jumped in his car, and backed out of the driveway. He started down the road, turned up his music, and continued to the new house. He pulled straight into the garage when he got there, and closed the door behind him. He walked into the house alone, and took a look around. He almost couldn't believe that he had a house just to store his kilos and mix up the work. Steve felt a momentary sense of pride in what he was doing. He nodded to himself as he took 10 kilos out of the guest room and placed them in his duffle bag. Things were coming together. Between the money coming in, and getting his credit fixed up, he could see a bright future in front of him. Steve caught himself daydreaming, shook his head, and walked into the bathroom. As he used the facilities, he looked around at the somewhat plain decor of the bathroom. Nothing was really old, it just wasn't necessarily nice and up to date. He thought about how if this was his place, he'd be replacing the kitchen countertops and cabinets, ripping out the bathtub and installing a nice tile shower, blowing out a wall to increase the size of the master bedroom, finishing the basement, and that was just the beginning. He checked his pants this time to make sure there wasn't any wet spots or have any reason for Angelia to question him. "I got real work to do right now and this ain't even gonna be my house for long the way things going," he said as he headed out the door into the garage, deadbolting it behind him. He then got the kilos situated in the stash spot. Steve looked over his shoulder before he backed out, turned up the music again, and made his way back to his house.

Angelia was standing in the kitchen fully dressed when he walked in. Steve could tell she took her time doing her makeup and doing her hair just right. "Damn! You so fine," he told her but, he could tell she still had an attitude from the look on her face. He thought about how pleasant his interaction with Shila just was in comparison to the tension he felt now.

"Thank you. Can you put it in my trunk for me?"

"Yea, I got you," Steve said as they walked into the garage and Steve placed the kilos into the trunk.

"Are you still going to Saginaw or you gone be here when I bring the money back?" Angelia asked as Steve opened the door for her, and they walked back into the house.

"I'll go tomorrow unless I can have him come down this way. I'll be here."

"Ok, I'll be back shortly."

CHAPTER
THIRTY

She left and drove to the hotel that they met at last time. While she was on the way, she thought about how she was getting an additional $10,000 as well just for this deal alone. As soon as she arrived, she texted Jon Jon to ask for the room number. He sent it to her, she got out and grabbed the duffel bag, and made her way to the elevator. The same bellhop that was there before recognized her and greeted her.

"Why hello again," he said with a smile. "Where are you headed to?"

"Third floor, please," she said, giving him a grin.

The elevator doors opened on the third floor. "Have a nice day."

"Thanks, you too."

She walked down the hallway to his room and knocked on the door. Jon Jon opened it right away.

"Pretty ass," he said with a smile before she walked in. "Come here." He picked her up with his good arm and closed the door as she wrapped her legs tightly around his hips. They tongue wrestled all the way to the bed where he let go of her, dropping her onto the bed. He gave her a menacing look, that let her know he might be a little aggressive. She hurried and removed her clothes, top and bottom. He grabbed her hips and pulled her to the edge of the bed as he started eating her pussy. He spit on her pussy, then began fingering her as he licked and sucked on her clit.

"Ouu, baby. Suck that clit," she moaned. Angelia looked around the room with her eyes half rolled back into her head from the pleasure. The room was very nice, with a formal, classy feel to it, but it wasn't the presidential suite by any means.

"Turn over," he said, roughly turning her over while admiring her yellow body that was perfect. He started eating her pussy from the back, as she arched her back, putting her ass up as far as she could with her face on the bed.

"Yes, baby!" she shouted, as she felt him continue to eat her out like a hungry lion. She let out a deep moan as she felt his dick slide all the way inside and then begin slamming in and out aggressively. Jon Jon began smacking her ass until it turned a fire engine red. Ever since she stopped him from using a condom, it was like he was trying to pound his dick into her chest. Every stroke was deep and powerful, but she loved it and took every inch until he grabbed her by the hips, pulled her all the way to him, and groaned as he came inside her.

Jon Jon pulled his dick out of her once he had released everything, and smacked her on her ass twice with his dick. She collapsed on top of the bed, laying there butt ass naked. Her body looked delicious against the white sheets. As he stood there looking at her, he could see the cum between her pussy lips while she laid there, sweating and breathing heavily.

CHAPTER
THIRTY-ONE

H e started going through the duffle bag she had brought. Everything was the same as last time, which made Jon Jon smile from ear to ear. He started taking the money out and setting it on the edge of the bed.

"I be missing your ass. We need to go to Jamaica sooner," he said, catching his breath and pulling his pants back up.

"I know, right. I be needing this dick like every night."

He laughed.

"Oh yeah? That's how you feel?"

"I swear, it be feeling so good." Angelia rolled over on her back and sat up slightly, holding herself up with her elbows. "You got me all tired now. I'm supposed to be meeting up with Esha."

"You good. Get your ass up and get your energy back, for I make you suck my dick."

She giggled. "I'll get up for that. Don't play."

They both laughed.

"This $340,000, well, $330,000, and $10,000 right here for you." He gave her a stack of hundreds. I appreciate the shit out you for this shit, real talk. Shit was kinda fucked up out here."

"You know I got you if I'm able to. No problem."

"So I heard you left with Kamozy after the club and shit."

"Just to go to the after party."

"Oh, that's all?"

"I mean, yea, we talked about stuff, modeling stuff. I'm supposed to do a photo shoot with him Saturday." Angelia had a flashback of Kamozy licking her ass, telling her she was going to be on his album cover.

"He funny. He want you to do a photo shoot with him?"

"Yea, he's paying me $1,500."

"He wasn't trying to fuck you?"

"Yea, he tried."

"Oh, ok. I figured that."

"Y'all cool or something?"

"Hell naw. I don't fuck with them niggas at all. That nigga a fake ass nigga."

"It's just business for me."

"I feel you. I was just asking because somebody had told me."

"Damn. They all up in my business."

"You was one of the coldest chicks in there. You know people was watching you. They can't help it."

"I see, ugh."

"So, what yo nigga been saying? He ain't mad at you no more or something? Your ass been out here."

She giggled, crossing her legs as she sat up a little higher. "He good. We fixed everything."

"That nigga ain't letting that good ass pussy go, huh?"

"Stop it. I'm a good woman too, especially when we on the same page. I explained to him how I was feeling when I cheated. He understood, so we good."

"That nigga love your ass. I woulda threw you out that window."

She giggled. "Shut up. What you have going on today?" she said as she walked to the bathroom to clean herself up and get dressed.

"Bouta go drop this shit off then I gotta pick up some money and shit, then that's about it."

"Well, I'm going to take a shower real quick, and go meet up with Esha. I'll call you later on. We may can meet up again. We going to be in the city."

"That's cool. I'll beat that pussy up again before you go home," he said as he peeked his head into the bathroom.

"Please do," she said as she turned on the shower. He admired her naked body and just watching her ass jiggle as she lifted up her leg to get into the shower made him want to go back inside her. He just shook his head, grabbed the bag, and put on his shoes.

"Holla at me later then," he said, closing the bathroom door.

CHAPTER
THIRTY-TWO

Once she was done showering she drove home, somewhat nervous with all that cash in the car. She glanced down at her gas gauge, hoping she had enough to get home without stopping. The dash showed 15 miles to empty. She let out a sigh of relief, put her hands at 10 and 2 on the steering wheel, and did the speed limit the whole way back. When she got there, she gave Steve all the money, and they both turned around and left, barely even giving each other much more than a hello. He needed to go over to the new house to stash his money and make up some kilos the way he wanted to put them out.

On the drive to the new house, Steve thought about the fact that if Angelia got all the kilos from him, he would only make a minimum profit. After he thought about the potential consequences, it didn't make any sense to him. He made a decision as he unlocked the door in the garage of the new house that he was going to remix everything. He locked the door behind him, and set the money bag on the counter in the kitchen. He leaned forward and thought for a minute.

Four and a half ounces were coming out of every kilo he got, no matter what. *I'm in this game to make money, not do favors*, he thought to himself. None of the buyers would know the difference anyway, since the starting quality was so good.

He had some guys he knew out in Grand Rapids that bought bricks, so he decided to give them a call. While he was on the phone explaining the situation to them, they were laughing, thinking he was joking. He immediately FaceTimed them, and they understood he wasn't playing. He told them to come out to see him with money for whatever they wanted to get. They told him they would come tomorrow at 5, with $45,000, which was a deal for them, especially considering the quality.

Don't do nothing over the phone, he heard in his mind. It was his uncle's voice. He reminded himself that he had to really be careful with that. The kilo price was high right now, and ounces were going for $1,700 to $2,000. Jon Jon, of course, was loving the price he was getting, and he was going to keep coming and buying as fast as he could, because he knew it could possibly stop or slow down in the future.

Steve had been working on the two tables in the guest room for hours, mixing and compressing everything all by himself. Luckily, he had Shila on the phone with him, which made the process seem effortless and fast. She had no idea what he was doing while she talked to him. She was just happy to be able to get some phone time with him. He planned to go see his uncle in the AM for about 2 hours. He wanted to ask him a few things, plus he wanted to buy more cut. As it got later and later, eventually Steve took a break, taking off his mask and gloves and thinking he would just chill on the couch for few minutes. He wound up falling asleep talking on the phone with Shila. By the time he woke up, it was 5 in the morning, and the phone was still on the line with Shila.

CHAPTER
THIRTY-THREE

"H ello, hello, hello," he said, but didn't get an answer from her, so he hung up. He looked at his notifications, and saw he had 60 missed calls, all from Angelia. She had sent 18 text messages, from love messages to hate messages. He tried calling back, but she didn't answer, so he hopped in the car to head home. On the way, he thought about what she must've been thinking with him not answering. His mind raced. He knew she was going to be pissed no matter what he had to say. As soon as he walked into the house, he saw his bags all packed up in the living room. It looked like everything he owned was in the pile of stuff.

"What the fuck?" he said as he walked up the stairs and saw her sitting in bed watching TV.

"Where were you?" she asked with a pissed off look.

"I fell asleep at the other spot, pressing and mixing -."

"Stop lying to me, Steve. Where the fuck were you?"

"What the hell wrong with you? I was just telling -."

"And you couldn't answer your phone! Really! Really! That's what we're doing now! Staying out all night and not answering our phones?" She got up and stomped her feet past him. "I'm not going to play these tit for tat games with you, Steve!"

"Calm down! The fuck is you talking about? I fell to sleep!"

"Whatever!"

"I'm not you. I don't have to lie about shit!"

"Let me see your fucking phone, Steve!" she yelled reaching for it, but he pulled it back.

"For what?"

"Let me see your phone, Steve. I'm asking nicely. You not about to play me like I'm one of these little bitches you be out here playing with!"

"There's no bitches. I fell to sleep. Do you know how much I had to do?"

"I don't care. I don't believe you. Let me see your phone!"

"Let me see yours too."

"Here!" She went and got it and handed it to him. He started looking through it, and she only had texts from family and friends he knew.

"You probably deleted shit."

"Your turn!" she said, holding out her hand which was shaking with rage. Her eyes were wild and her face was deep red in color.

He shook his head. "I'm not about to play with you. You tripping." He tried to walk away and she jumped on his back.

"Let me see if you wasn't with a bitch!" she shouted as she held onto his neck with one hand and punched him with the other hand.

"What the fuck is -," he said as he blocked her punches, walked her to the bed, and slammed her down. "Chill out. Fuck wrong with you! I told you I was at the other fucking house, you crazy ass bitch!" he said, realizing she had scratched his neck, leaving blood. Steve took a few steps back and grabbed ahold of his neck.

"Bitch!" she yelled as she charged at him again. She had a crazed look on her face, and was punching and slapping him. He just put his head down hoping she would stop. She didn't, so he picked her up and slammed her on the bed again.

"Chill out! What the fuck!"

"No! Get out!" she shouted. "Fuck you, Steve!"

He shook his head. "You are crazy."

"Get out!"

"What you mean, get out?"

"Leave. Your shit downstairs packed up! Leave!"

"Over what? The fuck -."

"Hiding shit, coming home at 6 the next morning!"

"So getting your fucking pussy pounded from the back ain't nowhere in that get out category?"

"Fuck you! Leave!"

"What the fuck did I do!" he yelled.

"Let me see your phone," she said, catching her breath.

CHAPTER
THIRTY-FOUR

S teve gave her the phone and she started going through his messages. Her hands were shaking as she began scrolling. Her jaw dropped and all she could do was break down crying with her hand over her mouth when she saw the texts from Shila, what they were talking about, all the lingerie and pussy pictures she had sent him, and the dick pictures he had sent her. After she had seen enough, she threw his phone as hard as she could at his head.

"I knew it, bitch!" she said with rage in her eyes. "I'm done!" She was crying and was so hurt she could barely yell. "You fucking this bitch, making love to her, eating her ass and her pussy. You a dirty motherfucker. I officially hate you," she said while looking him in his face, then pushing him out of the room. "Go. Just get out of here," she said as tears poured from her eyes. She slammed the door, and Steve's heart was in his stomach. He was hurt for her, knowing he hadn't ever deleted any of the messages. She saw all of it. He was sick, and he felt like a piece of shit. He went downstairs, plopped himself on the couch, and cried. About 10 minutes later, he looked up and saw Angelia coming down the stairs.

"Why haven't I seen or been to this new house? Is that where you bring her?" she asked as she started to get all worked up again. She stood in front of him with clenched fists while he sat on the couch.

"No, no. I didn't want you to want to move there. The place way bigger and better. I just . . ."

"Fucking liar! Wow!" She shook her head. "I want to go over there. Why the hell wouldn't you tell me? Am I your girl or your fucking side piece?"

"I'm sorry. I was going to tell you. I love you and only you, I swear. I'm so sorry. I did that shit out of spite." He got on his knees in tears. "Please, Angelia, forgive me. I'm so sorry."

She stared at him and felt like he was sincere, but her heart was broken and she was hurt. She just shook her head as she held her tears back. She wanted to kill him right now while he was on his knees. She was so mad. She looked at him in disgust. "You pick the Queen of Queen Whores to creep with on me? I cannot believe you. I'm sick to my fucking stomach. This bitch purposely did this. She hates me. You are a fake ass wanna be dope boy worker piece of shit. You can't fuck and you only good for eating pussy. I hope you die!"

Steve was hurt. That last comment cut him pretty deep. He had all kinds of thoughts racing through his head. He wondered how long she had been feeling like this. He also wondered why she was even with him still. He was beyond hurt and confused.

"Can you please forgive me? I'll do anything," he said, reaching out to hold her hands.

She pulled her hands away quickly and folded her arms. "Call this bitch and tell her you was only dealing with her because you was mad at me, and since you're not mad at me anymore, she don't exist."

"Can I just say I'm done with her?"

"NO!" she shouted. "You want me to write it down? Tell this bitch she's a losing ass bitch and you're done!"

"Ok, ok," he said, looking for her number on his cracked screen.

"Speaker phone!"

He put the phone on speaker as the phone rang, but there was no answer.

"Call back," she instructed.

He did, and Shila answered. "Hey, I was in the -."

"I'm done. I was only dealing with you because I was mad at my girl. Since I ain't mad at her no more, you don't exist."

"Loser bitch!" Angelia yelled as he hung up, not even giving Shila a chance to respond. Steve shook his head as he noticed Angelia grinning like she was happy.

"The only way I'm forgiving you is if you marry me. Otherwise, this is over. I'm done and not about to continue to play these games with you."

Steve was confused because of how badly she had just talked about him, and now she's saying he needs to marry her. "You're not happy with me. Why would we get married?"

"I am happy with you, if you don't cheat. It's the bitch you chose to cheat on me with. We're enemies."

"You just said I can't fuck and called me a fake wanna -."

"I'm hurt, Steve. I'm hurt. What the hell?"

"I'm sorry, Ang. I did that out of spite. I would never ever in a million years cheat on you, ever. She means nothing to me."

"You talked on the phone with her for over 7 fucking hours! About what?"

"I fell to sleep on the phone. We was on the phone for like an hour and a half, and that's only because I was mixing up the dope and shit. I was tired and needed to stay up. I didn't want to bother you because I knew you was out with your girl."

CHAPTER
THIRTY-FIVE

ngelia was so hurt and embarrassed. She did not think she would feel this way if Steve was dealing with someone else, but this one tore her up inside, and she realized her feelings were deep. She wanted to kill Shila inside, and wanted to hurt Steve as well. She couldn't believe what was going on, but she also felt like it was karma coming back to bite her.

"I don't want to do this, Steve, like I'm hurt . . . really hurt," she said as she broke down in tears again and tried to talk. "I . . . don't want . . . to play these back . . . and forward games . . . " she cried. "I will kill her. I swear to fucking God," she cried.

He grabbed ahold of her and looked her in her eyes. They both had tears in their eyes, and they both were hurting inside. "I don't want to play neither . . . I love you . . . You the only woman I ever loved. I swear to you, if you forgive me, I will do anything. I'm all about you. Whatever you want me to change, start doing, I'll do. If I got to watch pornos all day until I learn what you like, I will."

She giggled blowing snot on his arm. "It's not bad . . . like that, Steve."

"Just tell me what to do, and I'll do it. And I promise not to ever hurt you again." He was speaking in between tears and she felt his pain and her pain. She felt so bad for how she had been towards him, not knowing she loved him so much more than she had been showing him.

"I'm sorry, baby," he said, hugging and kissing her forehead. "I'm so sorry."

He held her in his arms and they both cried. They were so hurt and neither one of them wanted to let each other go. Imagining another girl with Steve was so far from what she wanted. Looking through his texts and seeing how much respect Shila had for him vs. the respect she didn't have anymore woke her up. Shila had been texting him sweet things all day, being very positive with him, and Angelia couldn't say the same about her own behavior. Steve's eyes were opened as well, because he saw the fire, the love and everything in Angelia that reassured him that he still had her heart. There were just some things he needed to work on, and he was willing.

"I'm sorry too, ok?" she said, squeezing a little harder and sniffling. She couldn't stop her tears from falling. She hadn't cried like this since she was a little girl, but it made her heart smile knowing she really did love him and want to be with him. They stayed glued together for an hour or so, hugging each other, and sobbing. It was like they couldn't get close enough to each other.

"Can we make this work?" he asked, looking at her in her eyes and wiping her tears away with his hands. She was looking back at him, still with her arms wrapped around him. Both of their eyes were red and watery. She shook her head yes, he planted a soft kiss right on her lips, and chills ran through both of their bodies immediately. He picked her up and carried her upstairs. The whole time her arms were around his neck while her legs rested in his left arm. She kissed him two times under his chin. She felt so secure in his arms. She had missed him so much. Although tears were still flowing out of her eyes, she felt like she caught her wind back and could breathe normally again. As they made it to their bed, they both laid down across it, looking at each other. He wiped her tears away again, and she wiped his back. Their eyes were locked and they both felt more in tune than they had been in years. Steve puckered his lips twice and she used her hand on the back of his head to pull him close to her lips and peck them softly, again and again.

"I love you so much. I never want to hurt you again, you hear me?" he told her.

She shook her head yes as two tears fell, one from each of her eyes. "I love you so much too," she said as she kissed him. She couldn't stop. It went from a long peck to sticking her tongue in his mouth. They began to tongue wrestle aggressively as both their hearts started to race. "I love you so much," she whispered, still kissing him like she was lost in ecstasy. "Can't nobody have you," she told him as she started taking her clothes off slowly.

CHAPTER
THIRTY-SIX

He started helping her with her clothes, and started taking his off as well. They came back together fast, locking lips all over again. It was like they were playing a game of who could stick their tongue further in who's mouth. He then began tongue kissing her neck, biting slowly on her soft skin, making his way down to her perky tits, and sucking on each nipple while gently massaging with his hand. "You love me, Steve?" she asked with her eyes closed, moaning and feeling the sensation of what he was doing with her breasts. He flicked her nipples gently with his tongue.

"I love you so much baby . . . so much," he said in between kisses as he made his way back to her lips. His body was pressed up against hers. She could feel his dick was hard, but went down to suck even more life into it, taking her time. She was anxious to prove to him that she was all he needed and she really did love him. She sucked and gagged on his dick like never before. She stroked and sucked nonstop, like she was trying to suck the cum out of him. She grabbed his hand, put it on her head, and pressed it. He took over and was pressing down until she couldn't breathe. "Aghh!" she said as her mouth went down for more. He started fucking her mouth, making his dick touch the back of her throat, choking her repeatedly, but she loved it and wanted more. She had saliva all over his dick and it was sticking straight up. She went down, licking and sucking his balls, putting one at a time in her mouth. He smelled so fresh as always; she had missed his scent. It was turning her on more and more as she heard him moaning while she sucked on each one of his balls.

"Yes, baby. Keep sucking them balls. That shit feel so good, baby," he whispered.

"You like that, baby?" She continued happily licking and sucking every inch of his balls. She raised his legs up a little as she licked under his balls, and lower as he propped his legs up for her, she licked the spot right between his ass and balls, and it drove him crazy. She then held his legs back as she kissed around his asshole then licked around it momentarily, then made her way back to his balls.

"Shiiit, baby," he moaned.

She started sucking and stroking his dick again. It was still insanely hard, and she could feel it jumping and throbbing. Steve wanted to please her now, so he grabbed her by her hair and threw her on her back. He spread her legs apart and put her arms over her head on the pillow. He dove his face into her pussy, striking her clit repeatedly with his fast-moving tongue. Her body stiffened up as she felt him pay close attention to the perfect spot. Her thighs started to shake as he kept licking, like he knew exactly what she was feeling.

"Oh! Shit!" She squeezed her eyes tightly as she felt her body about to cum hard. He kept going and going and soon, she was creaming hard. "Oh my goodness," she moaned as she spread her legs and patted her pussy twice. "Fuck me," she said in a raspy voice with a sexy look on her face. "Fuck me hard, baby."

Steve got on top of her and plunged his dick right inside her while holding her legs back. He started stroking faster and faster and faster. He thought about when he had caught her cheating, and that made him pound harder and harder, slamming his dick in and out of her pussy. He was giving it all he had.

"Yes! Papi! Si! Papi!" she shouted, realizing that something had clearly gotten into him. He was fucking her like he was mad at her, but she was loving every minute of it.

"Turn the fuck around," he said as he backed out of her and stared down at her with a wild look in his eyes.

"Ok, Papi," she said nervously as she rolled over, bent down, and arched her back. Before she was even comfortable, his dick was all the way inside her, hitting spots he knew he had never hit before. He was aggressive, doing every move he could think of, pissed off about earlier when she said he couldn't fuck.

"Ah! Ah! Ah! Ah! Ah! Papi! Ah!" she shouted as he pounded her pussy with force, gripping her waist and pulling her hips harder and harder towards him. "Shit! Papi, oh shit!" she screamed and stiffened up as she squirted, pushing his dick out, spraying all over the bed. He was surprised that she squirted. He had never seen her do that before. He wasn't done with her. He quickly grabbed her again.

"Come here," he said as he put his dick right back in and kept pounding the area that made her squirt and seconds later, she squirted again.

"Papi! Shit," she shouted, almost squirming to take a break, but he plunged back inside her pounding the same spot again and again. "Ah! Ah! Papi! I'ma squirt!" she yelled as she squirted all over him again. He pulled out and forcefully flipped her over, pushing her legs out to the side while sucking and licking her juices up. She was a swimming pool. Her juices were all over the bed, his legs, and his face. He licked and tasted every part of her. He picked her up while sticking his tongue into her mouth, giving her a taste of her own sweetness. He slid his dick inside her and started bouncing her in the air as she held onto his neck.

"Yes, Papi! Yes! Yes! Yes!" she shouted with each stroke clapping his hips loudly against hers. "You . . . fucking me . . . so . . . so . . . good . . . Papi . . . Yes!!!" she continued to scream after each stroke. His dick was rock hard, and she could feel him, gliding so good inside her she didn't know what to do.

He sat down on the edge of the bed, and she rode him as he squeezed her ass cheeks. "I love being inside you," he whispered as he felt her rocking slowly on his dick. She grinded on him as he pressed hard against her clit. "I'm about to cum, baby," he whispered, still moving her booty back and forth. He moved her hips faster and faster until he felt his cum shoot inside her, but she kept going as she was in ecstasy, eyes closed and moaning until she came as well, just seconds after him.

As they both slowed down and caught their breath, they were soaking wet with sweat. "I love you, baby. Let's start making babies," he told her, still inside her.

"Yes, anything you want. Twins if you want," she responded, kissing him again.

He laid back, collapsing on the bed tired and hot, and she laid on top of him. "I missed us," she said.

CHAPTER
THIRTY-SEVEN

"Me too, but we going to get back to us."

"We back," she said, raising her head up and looking at him. They both started laughing.

"Facts. We back. Who pussy is this?"

"Yours, Papi."

"You bet not give it to no one else."

"And you bet not give my dick to no one else, because it's mines right?"

"It's yours, baby."

"We getting your dick tattooed. I want my name on it."

He laughed. "That's gone hurt."

"I don't care. You can take the pain for me."

"Ok, I want my name on your pussy lips. I want the tattoo artist to flip one of your lips out and tat my name."

They laughed.

"Ok, not on your dick. On your neck."

"Well, you getting mine on your neck too."

"I'll get your name all over my body."

"Ok, I want it on your ass, neck, and thigh."

"You got it, baby. I'm all yours," she said, kissing him.

"If I ever catch you with another nigga, I'm killing y'all both."

"You won't see me with one, but if I see you with one or see another bitch on your phone, I'ma kill you then find that bitch and kill her too. Naw, I'ma kill her, not you. I don't want that bitch in heaven with you. You gone be in a wheelchair," she said, trying to make a mean look with her face.

He bust out laughing.

"So once I get this ring, and put it on your finger. You mine. Ain't no more game playing or you gone lose your life. I don't care how long I go to prison for. Just letting you know."

"So our marriage is a death contract, basically."

"Basically."

She giggled. "Deal." She kissed him, sticking her tongue back in his mouth. "I like how you was talking to me when you was fucking me and how rough you was. You made me squirt!"

"I know. I seen that. You knew you can do that already?"

"Yea, of course."

"Damn, why ain't you tell me?"

She giggled. "Tell you what?"

"That you can squirt."

"I don't know. I didn't think it mattered."

"Hell yea, it mattered. That's motivation. I'm trying to make you squirt every time."

"Please do."

"I see you like that rough shit, huh?"

"Yea, but not all the time . . . just most," she said, giggling.

"Bouta start beating your ass while we fucking now. It's on!"

"Shut up!" she said, giggling, forcing her pussy to fart. "Oh my God, your nut running out of me. Let me -."

"No, relax, baby. Just relax. I'm loving you laying on me."

She kissed him. "I love you baby. I'm going to love the shit out you."

"I'm going to love the shit out you back."

Angelia laid there on top of Steve. They could feel their hearts beating in unison. Their bodies felt like they were stuck together because of the sweat. He could feel his cum running out of her, dripping between his legs. Normally, he would want to get up and clean himself off, but he couldn't get enough of this moment; neither could she. Angelia propped herself up a little, and looked Steve into his eyes.

"I'm helping you from now on with all your cocaine stuff. I'll mix with you all night, right by your side. And whatever else you need me to do. I'm not sitting around anymore. You not leaving me at home anymore. I'm coming with you, even to your sells and all."

He laughed, playfully pushing her off him onto the bed next to him. He turned to lay on his side, holding his head up with his hand and looked at her. She looked so beautiful to him. He felt so infatuated with her. It was like it was when they first met. He remembered how he couldn't focus on anything except her for several months. He had planned his entire days around spending as much time with her as possible.

CHAPTER
THIRTY-EIGHT

"O k, baby. No problem. You can come with me from now on. And for the record, you called me a fake dope boy -."

"That's over with!" She tried to cover his mouth.

"Naw, naw, hear me out," he said, moving her hand smiling. "Hear me out. While you calling me a fake dope boy, I'm sitting on a couple hundred grand."

"Yea right. You just started. You don't have to -."

"Oh, you think I'm lying?"

"I know you're lying, Steve."

He laughed. "We going over to the new place today. I'ma show your ass something. You been sleeping on me, I see."

She giggled. "I have not . . . If you got a few hundred thousands, we getting married tomorrow," she joked. He grabbed her stomach and started tickling her.

"Oh, now you want me for my money!"

"No!" she giggled and screamed. "Stop! Ok! Ok!" she said, not able to stop laughing. "Ok, but I still want to see . . . This is after you pay your uncle, right?"

He laughed. "Oh you think it's a game, huh. You know your car paid off, right?"

Her mouth dropped open. "No . . . you're not paying a note?

"Hell naw. I cashed it out."

"Say, swear."

"Swear."

She looked at him to see if he would break and crack a smile. He didn't. "Stop playing, Steve!" she said in a playful way. "Stop trying to impress me. You know I don't care about that."

"Ain't nobody trying to impress you. I'm just telling you facts."

"My Cadillac is paid off, nothing owed?"

"Yes, Angelia. Where the fuck have you been?"

They both laughed.

"I swear you had a note. How much was it?"

"About 20 something."

She shook her head up and down. "I see you . . . I want to see this money we have, though."

"Oooh, WE now, huh!" he joked, attacking her again making her laugh.

"I'm going to shower. You coming?" she asked, getting him up out of the bed. "I can see my name on it right now, right there, going down," she pointed at his dick.

He laughed. "It's so tender there. That shit gone hurt on my dick, Ang."

"That's where I want it though," she whined.

"I'm getting yours all over me."

"When you getting off that birth control shit? I'm trying to make babies, like today," he said.

"Ouuu, cum in me, Papi," she moaned. "I'm joking . . . whenever is fine with me. I'll call and make an appointment today."

Angelia led Steve to the shower where they both got in together. They took their time soaping up each other's bodies and being playful. After getting out of the shower, they went back to the bedroom to get dressed. She called the doctor's office, and they told her she could come in today.

CHAPTER
THIRTY-NINE

After eating a snack, they jumped in the car to drive to the new house. On the way there, the sun was shining. The only clouds in the sky were light and wispy. It was a beautiful day. He held her hand as he drove, talking all about the new house the whole way there. She felt loved. As they turned into the subdivision, Angelia's jaw dropped.

"This is where it is?" she asked, shaking his hand up and down excitedly.

"Yea, this is the subdivision."

"Oh, wow. This looks like a nice neighborhood." They drove past a group of young kids having a squirt gun fight in a front yard. They chuckled together as one of the kids got sprayed in the face.

"It is. Good schools, too," Steve said while giving her a wink.

Angelia couldn't believe it as they pulled up to the house. Steve pulled directly into the garage, closing the door behind him.

"I can't believe this," Angelia said as she sat there impressed.

"Wait there," Steve replied as he walked around the car and opened the car door for her. He gave a slight bow, like a gentleman, then held her hand as he led her up the steps into the house. He unlocked the door, opened it, and jokingly held his arm out saying, "Behold! Our place."

It was just like James had said. Angelia immediately started talking about moving in. Steve told her to just wait, because something much bigger and better would be in the cards soon. He took her into the master bedroom first.

"Aww, you decorated the rooms?" she asked him.

"Yea, me and James just picked some shit out so the house wasn't vacant."

"So you ain't fuck that bitch on this bed then?"

"No."

"Promise?"

"Yes, I promise. Ang, we don't need to go through this again. We gone have a nice day."

"You right. I just couldn't help but make one comment," she said, giving him a playful push on the shoulder.

He took her into the spare bedroom, then took her into the work room. He showed her all the kilos he had, told her what he owed, and what his profits were. He showed her stacks and stacks of cash and she was amazed. At the same time, she couldn't understand why Steve continued to act the same way he did before he had money. He even showed her the access door to the attic, where he hid the extra coke he didn't need yet.

She was shocked seeing all that cash sitting there, and knowing he hadn't really spent any money on anything unnecessary. Angelia was the type of girl that wanted to take trips, shop all day, and live it up. She didn't understand why Steve wasn't ready to do the same. She began to ramble almost incoherently about taking a trip with her and going on a shopping spree, but he was patient with her, telling her that those days would come.

After they left the house, Steve took her to the doctor to get the birth control out of her arm. He brought her with him as he met his cousins in Detroit, and then to see Juice. He had to pull out the white Cadenza because Angelia hated riding in his Impala. They spent the whole day together, eating dinner at a high end restaurant in downtown Detroit, then went to a nice ice cream place and fed each other ice cream. Steve loved how easy life was with money. He didn't have to worry about budgeting or anything. He could get used to living this life without a care in the world.

CHAPTER
FORTY

Before they went home, she talked him into going to Sac's and buying her some high end designer wear with two purses. He spent $11,000 and she was happy. She sucked his dick the whole way home until he finally pulled in the driveway and came.

Tomorrow would be Friday, and they had plans to go get tattoos. Steve was loving every moment of his spending time with her. It felt so right to him. She was so beautiful to him both inside and out. Walking through the mall, his eyes stayed glued to her. He would even walk behind her just to see how her ass went from side to side as she walked in her heels. He loved how she got so much attention from the guys anywhere they went. Guys would always give him thumbs up when she wasn't looking, and that made him proud to have her. Plus, she was so touchy feely she was always trying to hold his hand or arm, or kiss him in the middle of the store or restaurant. She was always showing affection to him in public.

About 45 minutes after they got back to the house, Candy arrived. Angelia had told her she could stay with them for a couple months. Steve went downstairs while Angelia was in the shower.

He talked to Candy for a bit, saw what was going on, and slipped her $5,000, telling her to just stay tonight but to use that to get herself back together. He also instructed her not to tell Angelia he gave it to her. She agreed, accepting the money and giving him a hug. He wasn't sure why Angelia didn't want to help her, but he didn't care. He was in a happy place, and he didn't mind helping her.

Steve and Angelia made love most of the night, having sex all over their room while Angelia moaned loudly. Their antics kept Candy awake most of the night. Every time she came close to drifting to sleep, moans or banging would wake her back up. Steve was getting used to making Angelia squirt, and he was loving it. It was like he was able to hold his nut longer because he wanted to make her squirt at least a few times before he even thought about cumming.

Steve and Angelia had slept in until about 11 and Candy was gone. Angelia made breakfast, which they ate in bed while watching a couple episodes of Power. During the last episode, Steve started rubbing her thigh, which turned her on, and ended up causing them to have sex again before getting into the shower. After their showers, they drove together to the tattoo parlor. The whole way there, Steve joked about how bad his dick tattoo was going to hurt. He ended up getting her name on his chest, on his right pec, and she got his name on her thigh.

As Steve pulled out of the tattoo parlor and started driving down the street, he realized that today had been one of the best days him and Angelia had had together in years.

"I love you," he said as he glanced over at her in the passenger seat, looking so good to him.

"I love you more," she said, leaning over and giving him a kiss.

"You the only woman I want, you know that?"

"Aww, really?" she asked with puppy eyes.

"Yes, we stuck together forever."

"That's a fact."

"How's your leg feel after that tattoo?"

"Not bad. How's your chest?"

"It's a little tender, but I'm glad your name on it for good."

Angelia leaned to the side, resting her head on his shoulder, and let out a sigh. They spent the rest of the day together as he ran around town taking care of business. They were enjoying each other's company.

CHAPTER
FORTY-ONE

A s Steve drove, she was right there on his side texting Esha.

Angelia: I think I'm back in love with Steve.

Esha: You think bitch? Where you been these last few days?

Angelia: LOL I just told you. Falling back in love.

Esha: Stop playing with me.

Angelia: I'm not, look.

She sent a picture of both of their tattoos of their names.

Esha: Omg smh.

Angelia: What!

Esha: You are crazy. Why you get that boy tatted on you plus made him tat your name, when you know you don't want him no more?

Angelia: I do want him. And I didn't make him. I think it was actually his idea.

Esha: Are those real tattoos or are you messing with me?

Angelia: LOL Yes they are real. I'm off birth control and everything. Girl we bouta make babies, he gone put a ring on it too.

Esha: Wait...When did all this happen? I mean congrats. I'm def happy for you, but what just happened all of a sudden?

Angelia: Thank you...we just talked and I realized I still really loved him . . . ok let me be honest. Remember that bitch Shila?

Esha: No.

Angelia: Shila, the one I got into it with at Bar 7.

Esha: Ohh yea. What about her?

Angelia: Her number was in his phone. I guess they was talking.

Esha: Whaaatt!!!

Angelia: Yes, I snapped on his ass. Long story, I'll tell you tomorrow at the photo shoot. But that's when I realized I was still in love with him.

Esha: Lmao. Bitch! That don't mean you still in love. You just ain't want her ass to have him. And I was just about to ask you was your love bird ass going to the photo shoot tomorrow.

Angelia: LOL it do mean that. I'll explain tomorrow. Yes I'm still going to the photo shoot. I'll see you there.

Esha: Bitch whatever, I know you. You can't fool me. You bored with that nigga LOL. We will see.

Angelia: Bye hoe!

Esha: Lmao.

Angelia sat back in the passenger seat and fell asleep as Steve was still running around, back and forth, picking up money. The sun had dipped below the horizon by the time they got back. It had been a long day, but they had sex for hours, and went to sleep.

Angelia was up bright and early to get herself together for the photo shoot. She put on her favorite jeans that made her ass look super fat, heels, and a belly shirt. She was out of the house before Steve even woke up. It was nice and sunny out, and she was feeling herself as she looked at herself in the rearview mirror before backing out. She knew she looked good, and she was excited about the photo shoot. She sent Kamozy a text.

Angelia: Hey, I'm heading there now.

Kamozy: Perfect, can't wait to see you. Call me once you pull up.

Angelia: Ok, sounds good.

Angelia had her business face on. She decided to meet up with Esha so they could pull up together in the Range Rover. They met in the parking lot of a nice restaurant that was pretty close to the house in West Bloomfield. Esha pulled up about a minute after Angelia arrived. It was obvious Esha had just had it washed and waxed. The tires were wet with tire shine. Nobody could deny it was nice and clean, and it was showing off all it's beauty on this bright, sunny day. As Angelia stepped out of the car, Esha rolled down the window.

"You look cute," Esha said, tilting her head down and peering over her Prada sunglasses to check Angelia out. She had kept it simple, but was looking sexy as always.

"Thank you. Girl, you look cute too," she said, smiling. "Where's Candy?"

"She coming in about an hour. I wasn't about to wait," Esha told her.

CHAPTER
FORTY-TWO

A s they approached the address, they noticed the whole neighborhood was gated. Angelia called Kamozy as she pulled up outside the gates. He told her he would have the gates opened, and he was excited that she was there. As she hung up the phone, the two large, black, iron gates opened slowly. They pulled forward and looked around as a whole new world opened up before them. The first thing they noticed is that the houses were enormous. The homes were each spaced about a half mile apart, and each of them was strikingly unique. Many of them had the feel of small castles rather than typical residences. Passing by the cobblestone driveways with professionally designed landscaping, they couldn't help but turn their heads at all the brick, stone, fountains, and statues that came in and out of view.

"You have arrived at your destination," Siri said over the speakers.

"Oh my -."

"Girl, do you see this?" Esha remarked, taking off her sunglasses.

The circular driveway of the mansion was lined with Lamborghini's, Ferrari's, Bentley's, and Phantoms.

"Shit, girl, it's some real money in this mutha," Esha said in a high pitched voice.

"I see, damn," Angelia replied, trying not to sound nervous. She started breathing in and out slowly and deeply in an attempt to calm herself down.

"You ready to go fuck it up, bitch?"

"Yep," Angelia said as they saw Kamozy approaching them by himself. He opened the door, and took Angelia's hand as she stepped out of the car. He went in for a hug, and planted a kiss right on her lips before she could react.

"Hey, beautiful," he said with a big smile, showing off his bright white teeth.

"Hey, how are you?" Angelia responded, pissed she had just kissed him. It happened so quickly. It threw her off guard, and she was wondering what Kamozy might be thinking.

"I'm good, baby girl. What's up, Esha?"

"Hey, Kamozy." He walked over to greet her with a hug.

"Follow me, ladies," he said, leading them to the front door.

A porter opened up the enormous front door of the home, revealing quite a glorious sight to the girls. People were all over the place. The home had enormous windows, which allowed the whole home to be filled with an incredible natural light. They made their way through the home, being introduced to various influential people. The kitchen was set up with commercial grade appliances built for the home. A Sub Zero brand fridge and freezer were built into the wall, masked to look exactly like the mahogany cabinets. The countertops were a beautiful cream granite. The Wolf gas range had 8 gas burners with signature red knobs. The center island was massive, perfect for someone that loved to put out big arrangements of food for a large number of guests. The kitchen was open with an adjoining family room with remarkable views of the lake behind the home.

Esha and Angelia were treated like princesses by Kamozy all day. When he showed Angelia to her room, he had clothes all laid out for her. She recognized the makeup artist as one of the best in the industry. Angelia wasn't used to this level of pampering and special treatment. Throughout the day, she wasn't allowed to lift a finger to do or get anything for herself. Kamozy had everything both Esha and Angelia needed brought directly to them.

CHAPTER
FORTY-THREE

A week later.

Jon Jon had been trying to contact Angelia, but she wasn't answering or returning any of his calls or texts. After a while, he started to get seriously concerned that something had happened to her so he gave Esha a call. She told Jon Jon that Angelia was trying to work things out with Steve. Both of them had gotten new numbers, and to just give her space for the moment. Jon Jon was irritated because he felt like Angelia should have told him that was what was happening. What stung even more was the fact that he couldn't get kilos from her. She was the best source he had ever had. Nobody came close to bringing the quality through for the price he was paying, and Jon Jon had built up quite the demand. After talking with Esha, he was mad and couldn't calm down, so he called up a few of his homies and headed out to Pontiac.

Pontiac was not an overly large city, and after riding around for an hour, you'd generally see the same person a couple times. That's exactly what Jon Jon decided to do. Ride around the city. It didn't take long before he spotted Steve driving in his Impala.

"There he go right there," Jon Jon said, pointing.

"Where?"

"In that Impala?

"Yep. That's him."

All three of his homeboys laughed.

"Nigga, stop playing. I thought we was coming to get some bricks."

"That nigga got bricks. Fuck is you talking about? Follow him."

"Driving that?"

"Yea, nigga. Trust me, he got 'em. Y'all gone have to fuck the nigga up. Don't touch my bitch if she in there. Just throw her to the side or something."

Cam laughed. "Nigga, I'm not going in there being gentle with nobody. Everybody getting it if they have to get it. Fuck that bitch! She went MIA on you."

"You right. You right, but just try to, nigga. It's him with the money, not her."

"If that bitch try to come at me with something, I'm knocking her clean out, bro, no cap. We got this. We ain't gone kill your bitch."

They laughed and continued to follow Steve, keeping far enough back that he wouldn't notice he was being tailed.

They followed him around town for a few hours, watching his every move. They got to see him go where he slept, and even followed him to the stash house. They were both persistent and patient. All they needed to do was wait for the sun to fall. Jon Jon noticed Angelia's car parked at their main house, confirming she was there.

Cam spoke up again. "Nigga, I bet you the shit in that other crib. Don't look like nobody was living there."

"I'm with you on that. Let's hit that bitch first. Raymon, you gone have to cut the alarm and all that other shit."

"I got that. That's my specialty, cutting alarms and cracking safes, baby."

CHAPTER
FORTY-FOUR

L ater that night, Steve was drying himself off after a long, hot shower while Angelia was texting Esha.

Esha: Girl he really like you. What's wrong with you?

Angelia: Kamozy likes every girl he meets and wants to have sex with them.

Esha: Yea, groupies. He sees that you different. He serious about you.

Angelia: I'm not going for it. He just wants to have sex.

Esha: I think he likes you for real.

Angelia: Why?

Esha: I can just tell. Also, he ate your pussy. LOL I never heard of him eating none of these girls out. I had heard about him fucking and that's it.

Angelia: On the first night! I'm sure I'm not the only one. LOL

Esha: You got a point. I just don't want you to miss this opportunity. This nigga can really change your life.

Angelia: LOL I can clearly see that. But I'm focused on Steve right now. You see I'm not even dealing with Jon Jon ass.

Esha: Oh yea, he is pissed too. You coulda at least gave him some closure.

Angelia: Fuck him.

Esha: LMAO.

Angelia: Kamozy a cool dude, but he just used to having his way. He kissed me like nothing was wrong. That's why I hoed his ass later when he thought he could do it again. I'm like, 'Hold on, bud!'

Esha: LMAO Your ass crazy. Kamozy a good dude. He just likes you.

Angelia: I have a man. All we can do is business.

Esha: Well you seemed to be enjoying that lifestyle earlier.

Angelia: Facts bitch! I love it. But it's bad timing right now LOL.

Esha: Whatever bitch! You will come around. I'ma tell him to let you drive that Lambo. LOL

Angelia: LMAO!

Steve closed the bathroom door behind him, and turned off the lights. He ran and dove on Angelia. "Baby! I miss you!" he joked, kissing her to make her smile.

"Miss you too, boo."

"Where the drinks at? You slacking. What you was doing while I was in the shower?"

"Texting Esha's silly butt."

He laughed. "I'll go get them. Ice or no ice?"

"Ice, please."

Steve went downstairs, and got out the supplies to make them both drinks. He decided on Dusse and Coke for both of them. He came back into the room, and handed Angelia her drink. She thanked him and they clinked glasses and took a sip. Steve remembered he had something he wanted to discuss with her.

"Oh, so I went by the book store the other day and picked up this book on trucking called 'From Prison to the Car Hauling Game'."

"Sounds interesting. You want to drive trucks?" she asked, taking another sip of her drink as Steve took a seat next to her on the bed holding a thin book.

"Not drive them. I just want to buy some and have other people drive them."

"Oh, good idea. So what's the book about?"

"It basically shows you how to set your own company up. What I like about it, is that it's straight to the point. No extra, unnecessary fluff just to fill pages. The book is like 75 pages of pure gold. It's packed with all the info you need." He handed her the book. She accepted it, looking at the cover and giving a nod. She then proceeded to flip the book over and read the back cover.

"A. Roy Milligan was born and raised in Pontiac, Michigan. Oh wow, he's from here?" she said shocked. He grabbed the book back.

"For real? I probably know him. Let me look him up on FaceBook."

CHAPTER
FORTY-FIVE

S teve pulled him up on FaceBook, but realized he didn't know him. He noticed they had some mutual friends though.

"I know some of his younger cousins. I didn't even read the back. Here finish," he said as he gave her back the book.

"A. Roy Milligan was born and raised in Pontiac, Michigan, and started publishing books in prison while serving 4 1/2 years for selling drugs. He experienced a remarkable transformation that changed him from a drug dealer to a respected author. He wrote 'From Prison to the Car Hauling Game' to guide those who want to start their own transportation business. Sounds interesting," she said and then continued. "In this book, he provides a step-by-step guide for anyone to start their own transportation company. After reading this book, you will know just what to do to save time and money without making the mistakes most people make when they first start this business."

"Yea, I read it in like an hour, no lie. I think we should get some trucks."

Angelia was still thumbing through the book. "This pretty cool. I don't even know him, but I'm proud of him. Let me see his page," she said as Steve handed her his phone. *Damn, his ass was in prison,* Steve thought.

"He's a handsome dude. Looks like he's doing his thing," she said, scrolling his news feed. "He got other books too, babe. Ouu, I want to read this one, Women Lie Men Lie."

"Gimme my phone back before I fuck you up," he joked, taking back his phone.

They both broke out laughing.

"No worries, boo. I don't want nobody but you," she said, getting up and kissing him on his cheek. "So we getting into the trucking industry?"

"Yea, I'm thinking so. I'ma go talk to James about it because he has his CDL A already. Remember he used to drive trucks?"

"Yep, I do. I forgot he used to do that. Didn't he have his own or was he working for someone?"

"Working for someone."

"My dad used to drive trucks years ago, but it wasn't this car hauling," she said referring to the book.

"From my understanding, setting up the company and getting a semi is all the same thing. The trailer you buy will determine what you will be hauling. But setting it all up right is all in this book. So I'ma see what James thinks, and go from there."

"You're going to get one with a bed in it?" she asked, winking at him.

He smiled. "Yea . . . you trying to get fucked in the truck?"

She laughed. "I mean . . . why not?" she said with a little giggle.

"Your little freaky ass. Come here," he said, grabbing her and pulling her on top of him. He kissed her gently and looked her in the eyes. "I love your pretty ass. You so gorgeous. You know that?"

She smiled. "Thank you, baby. I love you too. My stomach always gets weak when you saying stuff like that."

He continued to kiss her, but more passionately, while rubbing nonstop on her booty, slightly massaging it. After a couple minutes, she felt his dick getting hard so she kissed him on the neck with juicy wet kisses, moving down to his chest, stopping to kiss on his stomach. She slowly pulled off his boxers, and began sucking his manhood nice and slowly. "Hold on," she said, reaching into the dresser and grabbing some little handcuffs with pink fur on them. "Cuff me. You're going to have to fuck my mouth since I'm going to be handcuffed," she said with a grin.

"Oh, I can do that." He got up and put the cuffs on her. "Stand up," he said yanking her hair kind of rough and throwing her into the wall. He went into character right away.

"No, Papi! Please don't take me to jail," she moaned, putting her hands behind her back, loving his roughness.

"Give me a reason why I shouldn't take your ass right to jail."

She turned around with the cuffs on. "Umm, I could suck your dick. If I did that, would you let me go free?"

"I'll let you know when you're finished," he said as he pushed down on the top of her head, causing her to drop to her knees. He started thrusting his hips, fucking her face while grabbing the back of her head by her hair. Saliva began to drip out of her mouth, as she gagged repeatedly on his dick. She loved how rough he had been playing with her lately. If she only would have told him before what she wanted, the sex would have been better long ago. She learned that she didn't even need to be direct and verbal, but could simply lead him with little physical cues. She began to communicate in creative ways, so he wouldn't feel offended. It worked every time.

"Get your ass . . . " he said pulling her by the hair. "Bend your sexy ass over." Steve pushed her from behind, bending her over the bed. "If you want to go free, you gotta give me some of that pussy. It looks like you might have some wet wet."

"Ok, Papi, but don't cum in me. I have a husband at home."

"Fuck your husband! I'ma buss all in that pussy," he said, ripping her panties out of the way, plunging his dick inside her soaking wet pussy.

"Please don't, Papi!" she shouted as he stroked her roughly.

CHAPTER
FORTY-SIX

Jon Jon and his homeboys had tore Steve's house up, and found 25 kilos in the attic. They also got their hands on stacks of money inside the safe they had broken into.

"You think it's more?" one of the guys asked.

"Hell, naw. This 25 bricks, nigga. I bet you this the whole bag. Let's get out this muthafucka," Jon Jon said with an excited and menacing look on his face. Neither the alarm nor the safe gave them any problems. The house was silent, and the neighborhood slept, never suspecting this was happening right on their street. They put everything inside a bag, and left the house.

After they got out of the neighborhood, they started yelling and screaming with joy. They drove back to Detroit, and stopped at a spot where they split everything up. Jon Jon, of course, took more than anyone else because it was his lead that got them the lick. As they were walking out of back door of the trap house Cam pulled out a .45 caliber Ruger and shot Raymon from behind. The hollow point ripped through the back of his skull, coming out the front, utterly destroying his face. Blood and brains sprayed all over the wall, door, and stairs.

"What the fuck!" the other guy said, hearing the boom and feeling the back of his neck sprayed with warm blood. By the time he turned around, Cam had the .45 pointed right at his face.

"Nigga, you know I can't be letting you both just leave with this dope."

"Nigga, please just -."

Boom!... Another round went off striking Ron in between the eyes and blowing out the back of his head. He collapsed immediately right inside the doorway. A large pool of blood started to form as both of their heads drained all over the white tile floor. Chunks of brain were splattered all over the back door, the wall, and floor. Cam picked up both duffle bags, and the sound of a door could be heard opening behind him.

"Bout time, nigga. I thought them niggas was really about to walk out of here with them bricks."

"Naw, I wasn't about to let that happen," Cam told him with a smile.

Jon Jon took the duffle bags from him, and they walked together back into the house where they split up the contents.

"Here. You take this 5."

Jon Jon kept 15 for himself, and 10 went to Cam.

CHAPTER
FORTY-SEVEN

T
he next morning, Steve was up bright and early. He got dressed, brushed his teeth, and left the house to go meet up with Juice to drop him off 10 kilos. Juice gave him $225,000 and was surprised to get an additional 5, but was happy.

"Hey, there was something I wanted to holla at you about, lil' bro."

"What's good?" Steve asked.

"It's some good work around right now. It's a little bit more expensive than this, but it's jumping back a little better. It's fish scales all through that shit. See if you can get something better. This tight though, don't get it twisted. I love this shit, but just see if your people got something better. That will make it easier for me. I could move more."

"Ok, I'll see what's up."

"Alright, bro. I'll hit you in a little while."

Steve hopped in his car and pulled off thinking about what Juice said. He decided he was just going to move it how he got it. No more remixing it. He wasn't even going to unwrap them. Plus, they had a stamp on them and Steve knew that's what he wanted for sure. He went and brought the money back to the house. He was getting close to having together what he owed Karo. After dropping off the cash, he made his way over to James' house.

"What's up with ya?" Steve said as he walked in the side door of James' crib. James had a blunt hanging from his mouth, puffing away while playing the video game.

"Chillin', chillin'. What's the deal?"

"Nothing much. I need help with starting a business. I want to get some trucks. You know this nigga, A. Roy Milligan?" Steve asked, handing him the car hauling book.

James looked at it.

"He from Pontiac," Steve added.

James shook his head. "Naw, let me hit Juice and see who he is."

James dialed his number and put him on speakerphone.

"Damn, I just left Juice. Didn't even think to ask him."

"What's up, lil' cuz?" Juice answered.

"What up doe? You know a nigga named A. Roy Milligan? I'm looking at his trucking -."

"Yea, yea, I know who he is. I don't fuck with him though. Why? What's up?"

"Steve just came over with a trucking book he wrote. I was just trying to see who this nigga was and if we knew him."

"Oh, yeah. He got a few books out. He official. He got the trucks and shit. He doing his thing. He showed one of my niggas how to get his trucking company going. The nigga did time and all that."

"Yea, it say he did 4 1/2 years. You said you don't be fucking with him?"

"Naw, I don't. I had a little, couple words with him. We be always fucking the same bitches. Remember the light skin bitch Sierra?"

"Yea, the bitch you was in love with?" James said and they both started laughing.

"Nigga that was my bitch, but I guess her and the nigga was best friends or some shit. I ain't like that shit. I felt like the nigga was fucking the bitch, and he said naw, they wasn't like that, but I ain't believe neither one of they ass. That nigga be running through shit out here. I know they fucked."

James and Steve were laughing.

"For real, that nigga a sneaky dick ass nigga. I just cut that bitch off like, I'm cool on you."

James laughed. "Why you ain't just tell her she couldn't be friends with him no more?"

"Shit, I basically did, and this bitch was like, that's not fair along with all this other sentimental shit. Protecting the nigga, basically."

James laughed again. "Say, she said, my bestie ain't going no where, huh?" he joked.

"Man, for real. I'm like what kinda shit you got going on, bitch. I'm gone. Bitch was cute and shit but I ain't playing them best friend games with none of these hoes out here."

"I feel you. Me neither. Best friend my ass. I wish Eboni would come home talking about best friend. That nigga better be gay."

They all started laughing.

"So you stop fucking her because Roy had his grips on her."

"Yea, the nigga voodooed my bitch or something. I had her pregnant and all. I aborted that baby. I don't know what the fuck was wrong with that bitch." Juice started laughing. "Who about to start a trucking company?"

"Steve."

"Oh yeah? That's what's up."

"Alright, nigga. I was just calling to see who dude was."

"Yea, he cool. He know what he talking about. Tell Steve just to follow that book."

"He hear you. You on speaker."

"Good looking, bro," Steve said.

"Fasho, holla at me."

James hung up.

"So, yea. How you set up your business?" Steve asked.

"I went through Legal Zoom. They did everything for me for like $500. All I needed to give them was the name of my company, my address, and all that. They filed the paperwork for me and got me a LLC. You can do it cheaper, I heard, but I don't know how and didn't want to take the time to figure it out."

"Naw, I'll pay them. I don't wanna figure it out neither."

"You got a name for your company?"

"Hell naw, I'ma have to think of something."

"Shit, let me know when you do. I got my guy on speed dial, the dude that did all my shit."

"Ok, bet."

"You trying to get whooped in Madden right quick?"

"$500, you don't win," Steve said, digging in his pocket.

"$100."

Steve laughed. "Alright, $100."

He stayed over chilling with James for a few hours until his phone rang. It was the twins calling to tell him they were ready for some more coke.

"Alright, bro. I gotta go handle some business," Steve said, giving James a pound and heading out the door.

"Fasho. Get at me later."

CHAPTER
FORTY-EIGHT

Steve was excited as he was heading to the stash house. Business was going good. He pulled into the driveway as usual, and walked in the house. His heart dropped. He could instantly tell what had happened. The whole house had been torn apart. The cabinets were all open, with drawers thrown all over the floor. The fridge was knocked over, and the microwave had been ripped off the wall. The couches were flipped upside down. He looked up in the corner of the living room, and saw the cameras had been ripped down, and the wiring was burnt. Even the vent caps in the floor had been pulled out. The mattresses were off the beds, and the pillows were all cut open. Steve's heart started to pound faster and faster. Sweat began to form on his forehead. Anger and despair consumed him. The carpet had even been ripped back. His mind started racing, and he thought about his safe. When he opened the door to the room with the safe in it, he started shaking, and his legs got weak. The door on the safe was open, and it was empty. *You gotta be fucking kidding me*, he thought as he made his way to the access to the attic. He saw the access door pushed to the side, and he dropped to his knees. He didn't need to go up there to know that the kilos were gone. As he got back up to feet, the feeling of despair began to be replaced with burning anger. He checked, and the kilos were gone. Other than the house being torn apart, this looked like an inside job. The safe door was just open, like someone knew the combination. He wondered if his mom, James, Angelia, or his uncle had anything to do with it, but he wasn't going to jump to any conclusions. Steve decided to drive back to James' house to tell him what had happened.

Steve walked in the door, and collapsed on James' couch. He told him what he found at the house.

"You know I would never pull some shit like that, bro. And I can assure you my uncle didn't have anything to do with it."

"Yea, I feel you. I know you ain't have nothing to do with it. Damn, man! This shit fucked up. I owe a lot of money to this fucking plug. Fuck!"

"I got a few thousand if you need it, bro."

"Nigga, I owe over a million. I gotta go home and see what I got. Fuck!"

Steve got up and ran out the side door and drove home. His hands were shaking the whole way there, and the feeling in the pit of his stomach wouldn't go away. He stormed into the house and ran right past Angelia who was Snapchatting.

"What's wrong?" she yelled behind him.

"A lot! I need to count this money. Box up both them Rolex watches. They gotta go back. I gotta pay this plug." He was talking fast, rambling on. His movements were frantic as he started running stacks of cash through the money counter, praying it would come close to the $1.8 million he owed.

"Ok, baby. Relax. You scaring me."

"It's ok. I'm good. It's ok. Don't be scared," he said, trying to control himself. He continued running money through the counter. It totaled $1.2 million. Angelia was shocked. She had no idea that much money was in the house. He kept pulling stacks of money out from random places.

"Damn, I'ma be a couple hundred short. I can get that. Fuck!" he said as he finally sank into a chair to catch his breath. His clothes were drenched in sweat.

"Good, baby, good," she said, trying to keep calm herself while calming him down. She didn't know what to say. She was really just hoping he could pay his tab, because she was sure at this point he was in with some people that wouldn't play games with their money. She didn't want to go through the same things she remembered going through with her father. Although she loved her new car, she was willing to give it back.

"Somebody got me good. They took all my shit. What the fuck?" he said, trying to figure it all out.

"You think it was someone you know?"

"The only people that knew about the house were James, mom, James' uncle, and you. James didn't seem like he had anything to do with it. He said his uncle would never. My mom would never, although she was the first person to come to mind because of the safe."

"Don't be silly. She'd never do that."

"I know. I know."

"You think maybe somebody was following you?"

"I'm sure I woulda noticed that."

"Not in this little ass city. It's Pontiac. You can get followed on a bike up in this little ass place."

CHAPTER
FORTY-NINE

S teve thought about it for a minute, replaying the events of the previous day in his mind. Somebody following him was the only scenario that seemed to make sense. It still didn't explain the safe, but he knew there were professionals that could do that kind of thing. He was ready to move out of Pontiac, and start playing his cards totally different. He started calculating what was owed to him.

After he returned the watches, got his money out of the streets, and sold Angelia's car, he was still going to be a little short. He wondered if Juice might want to pay him up front for a couple. That could make up the gap in what he owed. He called up Juice. He was more then willing to help him out. Juice told him to come and get it any time over the weekend.

The rest of the week dragged on and on. It seemed like the weekend couldn't come fast enough. Steve still couldn't put together who it was that broke into the house. He got together with James' uncle and explained to him the situation, letting him know he wanted to move out. His uncle was very understanding, and told him he'd just have to give up $2,500 for getting out of the lease early.

As Steve went around collecting the money he was owed, he started to think differently. This was a big loss, and he never wanted to go through that again. He didn't trust anyone at this point. The incident could have resulted in the loss of his life and the lives of the ones he loved.

Karo's next drop was 250 kilos of cocaine at $28,000 a piece inside the back of a one year old Ram truck, with a hard top cover over the bed. It wasn't stashed this time, but Steve didn't care. He was happy to have product back in his hands. He started calling everyone he knew. Angelia was dropping off bricks in the white Kia, and he was using the Impala.

By the time 3 weeks had past, he had sold plenty. Everyone was loving this new shit. He wasn't cutting it at all, and people could see the stamps on the kilos when they got them. He had guys in Grand Rapids, Flint, Saginaw, Redford, Detroit, Pontiac, Pennsylvania, Alabama, and Tennessee. He was trying to expand fast, and it was happening. Everyone who sampled it wanted as much of it as they could could get. Nobody could get enough. He started charging $38,000 across the board, no matter who you were. Of course, nobody was complaining. He had by far the best quality coke at the cheapest price. There was no competition.

It wasn't long before Steve called CeCe and had her scope out a house for him on Williams Lake in a city called Waterford, which was not too far from Pontiac. It was far enough out for him to feel safe, but close enough for him to still be able to get to the city fairly quickly. CeCe found him a 4 bedroom, 3 bathroom lake front home to lease with an option to buy. Angelia absolutely loved the place. She was itching to get everything decorated the way she wanted, but Steve had her wait until Karo was taken care of.

About three weeks later, he was sold out again. Things were moving fast, and the money was piling up. Dropping the price while delivering his customers pure, stamped, uncut coke was the best thing he did. Everyone that was moving his stuff around was eating good. Soon, Karo contacted him for a face to face meeting and flew him into Mexico City, Mexico. Angelia was excited to stay home, shop, and decorate the new house, plus she had her another Cadillac.

CHAPTER
FIFTY

A couple days later.

Shila had been trying to get in touch with Steve for weeks now. She was pissed off he just went cold turkey on her like that. He had blocked her on his phone, and wasn't answering the blocked calls. She was just getting back into the U.S. after a 2 week vacation with her mom, a few friends, and her kids. She was devastated that Steve didn't even attempt to reach out to her, not even once. She knew he was in love with Angelia, and she didn't like it. She felt that Angelia didn't deserve a good guy like him. Shila decided it was time to show Steve what kind of girl Angelia really was.

Shila had messed around here and there with her baby daddy, but she had made a promise to stay away from him because he was addictive to her. Time and time again she would get sucked back in. This time though, she had plans. She began texting him all day, telling him all about the trip, and sending him pictures of her in her bathing suit. They had a good relationship as far as parenting goes. This last time before he got locked up, they had been messing around, having sex, and talking about being together, but nothing ever materialized. He just had too many women around to stay loyal.

After texting him all day, Shila showed up at his house in Southfield. He had a very nice 4 bedroom home in a quiet neighborhood.

"What's up, sweetheart?" he said, opening the door. Shila was dressed in a pea coat with nothing underneath it. Before heading over there, she had drunk a few shots. She didn't respond when he opened the door. She closed the door behind her, got on her knees, and started sucking his dick. It swelled up pretty quickly, and she kept going, gagging and slobbing all over him.

"You miss this dick, huh," he said, taking it out of her mouth and smacking her in the face with it.

"Yes. Give it here," she said, putting it back in her mouth and sucking on it again while moaning. He grabbed the back of her head, and pulled her as close as he could, trying to slide his dick down the back of her throat. It wouldn't go. She started choking and almost threw up.

"Ahh," she gasped. He smacked her a few times, bent over to kiss her passionately, backed off, then spit in her mouth.

"Swallow it!" he demanded, then smacked her again. "Stand up," he said, jerking her up by her arm and pulling her into the kitchen. He pointed to the island with the granite counter top. Before her foot was even up there, he was already inside her, pounding away with three fingers in her mouth, pulling her bottom jaw into her neck.

"Ah, shit! Shit! Shit!" she screamed as she felt him pounding her aggressively. She hadn't been having sex with anyone his size in quite some time. Although he was only a touch thicker, and about 2 inches longer than Steve, it felt like a big difference because he was so aggressive.

"Ace! Ace! Baby!" she shouted in between every stroke. Nothing had changed with him. He always fucked her like he was making a porno. Although she genuinely missed him, she was there for a purpose. She knew he always recorded himself having sex, and her goal was to find the clip of him having sex with Angelia, and get it to Steve.

Ace fucked her for 45 minutes straight, all over the kitchen and living room. By the time he was done with her, she was drenched in sweat with her makeup smeared everywhere. She stretched out on the couch, gasping for air. She was finished. Her whole body felt abused.

"You just killed me," she said while she felt the semen run out of her pussy. There was nothing she could do. She couldn't move.

"I'm not done with you neither," he told her as he got a big jug of water and started drinking, like he just ran a marathon.

Later that night, they had sex again, and Ace recorded it. He still had his cameras set up just like she remembered. He was making her pay, exhausting her and working her out. In her mind, she just kept focused on her mission. She was leaving the house with that SD Card. After he came again, he was ready for bed, but Shila began to execute her plan.

She ran to the bathroom. "Oh my God," she yelled.

"What?"

She shut the door behind her and let the nut run out of her into the toilet. "Damn!"

"What's up, sweetheart?"

"My period coming. You have some tampons or pads here? You made it come."

"Oh, damn. You ain't got none in your purse?"

"I'm not supposed to start until next week. Can you grab me some?"

"Yea, no problem. I got you." He got dressed and ran up to a nearby store.

Shila went straight to searching through his stuff. She went through everything and found nothing, so she went to his closet. After opening up a handful of boxes, she found them. All of them had names written on them. She saw "Ang" written on three of the cards. "Bingo!" She took all three, tossed them into her purse, then put everything back in place.

CHAPTER
FIFTY-ONE

Steve woke up to a knock on his hotel door. Karo had him set up in one of the best hotels in Mexico City. He was on the 20th floor with a beautiful view that overlooked the city. Steve glanced down at his phone as he walked to the door. It was 9:00 AM. He glanced through the peep hole and it was Karo along with a white gentleman he hadn't seen before. He opened the door up, and Karo wrapped her arms around his neck, hugging him and kissing both of his cheeks.

"Hola," she said, after letting go of him. "This is John. He is a good friend of mine who I wanted to introduce to you. He is a specialist in all things when it comes to business. John, this is Steve."

They shook hands and greeted each other. "He's a lender and I want you guys to work together to clean up some of your money. He has his hands in many buckets, but specializes in real estate. He can help you out. You'll do your financing through him, since you don't have a business up and running yet, which brings me to my second point. I need you to open a legit business. Bringing in the money you are, you'll need it. John can help you with that as well."

"I appreciate the offer to help. I been looking into the dump truck business, and have been thinking about purchasing a few trucks," Steve replied.

"Good, good. I don't want you going to jail," Karo said. She loved the work he was putting in and appreciated his loyalty and discretion.

Steve's notification went off. James had just sent him a TikTok video. It was Angelia doing the buss it down challenge. Seeing the video got Steve irritated.

"Everything ok?" Karo asked.

"Yea, yea. It's nothing. I just have to send a quick message to my girl if you don't mind," Steve said as he pasted the video link into a text message to Angelia.

"No worries. Relationships are important," Karo told him.

Steve: What the fuck is this?

Angelia: A challenge . . .

Steve: Smh look like some thot shit to me.

Angelia: Relax. Everybody is doing it.

Steve: I ain't feeling that shit.

Angelia: Loosen up. It's not that serious.

Steve: It's very serious. You want me to marry you and you shaking your ass all over the internet. Wtf.

Angelia: It's a challenge, gosh!

Steve: Gosh my ass. Take that shit off. I don't like it.

Angelia: You tripping for no reason. All the grown and sexy is doing it.

Steve: Whatever, Angelia.

Karo noticed he seemed upset, and was about to say something as Steve looked up and put his phone away.

"Sorry about that," he said, taking notice of the look on Karo's face.

CHAPTER
FIFTY-TWO

K aro picked up the remote control and turned on the 55 inch TV mounted to the wall. Steve's eyes widened as he looked at the TV screen.

"Missing any kilos lately?" Karo asked as Steve recognized Jon Jon on the screen, strapped to a stainless steel table elevated at a 45 degree angle with his face badly bruised and bleeding. His body was secured to the table with shrink wrap. He had bands of it across his head, chest and arms, and legs. He couldn't move at all and his mouth was covered in duct tape. He was wearing no clothes except for a pair of boxers and a white tank top, covered in blood and torn apart. Four guys were standing beside him, two on each side. All of them wore black ski masks with cowboy boots, jeans, and large belt buckles. Three of them held guns to Jon Jon's head while one of them stood there with a pair of tree pruners in his hand, the kind used for lopping off branches. It looked like they were in some kind of abandoned warehouse. The only light in the room came from a yellow metal work lamp, the kind you see on construction sites.

"This is the guy who took the kilos you're missing. You know him?"

"Um . . . yea, no, not really," Steve answered nervously. His heartrate was increasing steadily and his throat had dried up. He couldn't believe what he saw before his eyes.

"Um . . . my . . . girlfriend does. I don't."

"Oh, she does? You think she put him up to this?"

"No, not at all."

"Good," she said.

The man with the tree pruners took a step closer to Jon Jon. He began wriggling and squirming, trying to talk through the duct tape. He was saying Steve's name.

"He can see me?" Steve asked, turning his head to look at Karo.

"Si."

Steve was speechless. He didn't know what to say. The man with the pruners lopped off Jon Jon's thumb. He squinted his eyes in pain and let out a muffled scream.

"Gentleman, I want him to have to look at Steve," Karo said as she looked at the TV.

One of the men responded, "No problem." He pulled out what looked like a pair of needle nose pliers and a box cutter from his pocket. Using the pliers, he pulled Jon Jon's upper eyelid away from his eye, and removed it carefully with the box cutter. He did the same to the other side. The sight, along with the frantic screams and panic, caused Steve to become nauseous, but he didn't dare say anything.

Blood ran down from where Jon Jon's eyelids used to be and screams could be heard as each finger fell to the floor as they clipped one after another. Steve couldn't look anymore. Karo stared at the screen, enjoying the retribution, as John, her business specialist, looked away. He didn't have the stomach for that kind of thing, but seeing it was nothing new to him.

Karo muted the TV. "Did you know he had stolen from you?" Karo asked.

"Yea, I knew somebody did, but I didn't know who it was."

"It was him and three of his buddies. Two is already dead. This one will be soon, and then we will follow up with the other guy. I have eyes and ears everywhere, but I'm going to need you to protect yourself better and not be so loose about things in the future. This is a serious business. It's very serious to me and my family. You understand?"

"Yes, I understand."

"That could have been you in that chair if you wouldn't have paid me my money. You understand?" she said with her eyes still plastered to the events on the TV.

Steve gulped. "Yes, I understand. It won't happen again."

"Good boy," she said as she turned around to face Steve, and unmuted the TV. All of Jon Jon's fingers and toes had been removed. One of the men had stepped off screen and returned with a chainsaw. He started it up and began removing Jon Jon's limbs. As he sawed off each limb, blood sprayed all over the men. The chainsaw cut through his limbs like butter. As his second arm was being removed, he went limp and his head rested on his shoulder. The sound of the chainsaw tearing through flesh and bone continued in the background as Steve and John kept their eyes looking anywhere but on the screen. The men in the room with Jon Jon seemed to enjoy what they were doing. At this point, Jon Jon's body was lifeless, but the chain sawing continued. Karo turned the TV off.

"You won't see him again. 300 kilos will be waiting for you once you get back."

CHAPTER
FIFTY-THREE

A week later.

Esha was picking up Angelia to go shopping with her and to catch her up on the news. Angelia came outside walking in a pair of white stilettos, blue denim skinny jeans, and a white blouse. "Hey, girl," she said as she got in.

"You look cute," Esha said as she looked over her shoulder to back out the driveway.

"So is this shit really true about Jon Jon? I literally cried all night."

"Yes, it's true. They did him so wrong."

"What happened?"

"He was kidnapped by some people wearing all black with ski masks and big ass guns. People said they looked like a SWAT team the way they jumped out and came for him. A couple days later, his mom received a package. When she opened it up, she screamed as she saw her son's head with his eyes and tongue missing."

"What the . . . " Angelia said, covering her mouth in terror.

"I know, right? Sent this nigga head, girl. I ain't never seen or heard no shit like that in my life. Like damn, you had to do all that to him?"

"Damn, girl."

"His mom had a stroke a few minutes after she opened the box. The following day, his limbs were sent to his baby momma's house. They cut that boy up into pieces. It's unreal."

"Oh my God! No," Angelia said through tears.

"I don't know what he was into or what he did, but he crossed the wrong people for sure. It wasn't a robbery either. They sent all his money and jewelry back too. This was revenge for something. That jewelry was worth money."

"Lord, Lord, I can not do this today," Angelia cried out as she fanned herself. Every time she thought about Jon Jon, more tears fell. She started to regret blocking him and cutting him off.

"Girl, the streets is so mad right now. You know Jon Jon was feeding a lot of guys in Detroit and now that nigga is really gone."

Esha shook her head in disbelief, as tears rolled down her face too.

"He must was messing with a cartel. That's some cartel shit. Trust me on that one."

"You think so?"

"Yes! I do. He must've fucked them over or something."

Esha shook her head and thought about what Angelia was saying. She had no clue who could have done it, and Jon Jon's people were clueless too. They all knew that Jon Jon wasn't linked up directly with a cartel, so none of this made sense.

By the time they arrived at Somerset Mall, they both had dried up their tears and were ready to drown their sorrows with some shopping. Angelia was still a little puffy in the face. "Damn, girl. I didn't even tell you . . . Look!" Angelia said, holding out her hand, showing off a new engagement ring. "I said yes!"

"Bitch!!! Congrats!!! Oh my God, that ring fire!!!"

Esha gave her a big hug. "We gotta celebrate this tonight. We turning up!" Esha screamed. Angelia was cracking up.

"Let's tear this mall up!" Angelia said.

"Let's!"

CHAPTER FIFTY-FOUR

A few days later, Steve rolled over and stretched his arms over his head. He let out a big yawn and looked over at the clock. It was only 7 in the morning, but the smell of bacon, eggs, and pancakes filled the air, motivating him to get up. He climbed out of bed in his boxers and put on a t-shirt before walking downstairs. As he walked into the kitchen, Angelia was putting together a plate of food for him. She set it on the kitchen table. Steve looked her up and down. She was wearing an all black dress with black high heels, and had clearly already gotten herself together for the day. "Where you going?" Steve asked, as he sat down at the table and took a big bite of a pancake after dipping it into syrup.

"A funeral. Esha asked me to go with her. I forgot to tell you."

Steve thought for a moment and he chewed. Jon Jon crossed his mind. "A funeral? Where at?"

"I think it's somewhere in Detroit. You want apple juice or orange juice? I have time to make some coffee too if you want before I go."

"I don't need any coffee. Just orange juice is good." Angelia walked over to the fridge and got out a jug of orange juice. She filled him up a cup and set it down in front of him. When she set it down, Steve noticed she didn't have her ring on.

"Thanks. You're not wearing your ring today?"

"Yes, of course I am. I will never leave the house without it, Papi," she said as she leaned in put her hands on the sides of his face and gave him a loud, exaggerated kiss before walking into the bedroom, putting on the ring, and coming back. Although he wanted to believe her, he was still suspicious. Steve took out his phone and texted James telling him to follow Angelia around today, and he would pay him $1,000. He had a bad feeling, and he thought the peace of mind that would come from knowing her whereabouts would be well worth the money. He really wanted to trust her, but this was just too big of a coincidence for him to ignore.

"What time will you be back?"

"I'm not sure. I'm going to be with her as long as she needs me. She's been taking this one pretty hard." Angelia grabbed her keys off the counter and put them in her purse.

"Damn, that's messed up. I feel bad for her. Tell her I'm praying for her to have strength." Steve took the last bite off of his plate and stood up, walking his plate over to the sink.

"I will."

"You look beautiful by the way," Steve said, turning around to look at her.

"Thanks, Papi."

"You welcome." He tried to keep a calm look on his face, but the thought of her going to Jon Jon's funeral haunted him. He wasn't even sure if that's where she was going today, but he was going to find out either way. As she turned to walk out the door, he admired the way her ass was switching from left to right. "Damn, you so sexy," he said, shaking his head.

She turned her head around, looking back at Steve over her shoulder. "And I'm all yours," she said as she pointed at him, giving him a seductive look.

"Come here. Let me hit it from the back right quick before you leave."

She giggled. "Can you wait until I get back, please? I don't feel like jumping in the shower again. Plus, I'm already running late."

"Damn, you just going to turn down your husband like that?"

"Steve! Stop it! Why are you messing with me like this? I gotta go."

"I'm not messing with you. I want some of that pussy. Come give me some."

Angelia could tell by the tone of his voice and the look in his eyes that he was dead ass serious. The way he said it made her feel like she had no say in the matter. It turned her on, and she spun all the way back toward him, walking up to him without saying a word. She pulled his boxers down as she bent over in front of him and put his dick in her mouth. She started to suck it while stroking it slowly. Steve let out a soft moan and said, "Yea, leave them heels and that dress on. I wanna fuck you in this dress. You wearing panties?"

"Yes," she said with his dick still in her mouth.

What Angelia was doing felt good to him, but he was distracted and getting more and more irritated because he felt in his heart that she was going to Jon Jon's funeral. He just knew it.

"Why you not getting hard, baby?" she asked while still stroking and sucking.

"Keep going. I will be in a sec." He was going to have to clear his mind if he was going to be able to enjoy himself, so he took a deep breath and tried to let it all go. It worked, and soon, he was rock hard. "Turn around," he instructed her. She did what he asked and he stood up, pulled her panties down, and lifted her dress all the way up so he wouldn't get anything on it. He smacked her ass hard, then jammed his dick insider her and began pounding her from behind. He wanted to choke her, pull her hair, and be really rough with her, but he knew now wasn't the time since she was on her way out the door.

"Ouu shit, Papi!" she shouted as he continued to pound away at her aggressively, using her waist for leverage. "Si! Si! Si! Papi! Si!"

Sweat dripped from his forehead as he pounded away repeatedly as hard as he could. "Damn, Papi!" she shouted, still taking his dick, stroke by stroke. "Don't stop, Papi! Don't stop!" She felt his thumb slip inside her asshole and it turned her on even more as she grew closer and closer to an orgasm.

"Oh my God, I'm about to cum!" she moaned as his hips hit against her ass hard and fast while he was still stroking. Different thoughts continued to pop into Steve's head which caused him to last much longer than usual. He had no intention on cumming any time soon, and Angelia was loving every minute of it even though she really had to go.

Steve continued to put in work on her, making her cum twice. After about 30 minutes of fast, followed by slow, hard pounding, he exploded.

"Oh, shittt. I'm cumming in this shit, baby!" he growled as sperm shot out of the end of his dick, filling the deepest places inside her pussy. "Shitt!" he said, throwing her off him and sinking back into the chair.

"Ok, you . . . can go . . . now," he said, getting out each word in between deep breaths.

CHAPTER
FIFTY-FIVE

She grabbed a paper towel off the counter, ran it under warm water, wiped herself off, and pulled up her panties. As she straightened up her dress, she looked at him and said with a smile, "So you just gone fuck the shit out of me like that, and send me on my way, huh?" Her legs were a little wobbly as she continued to straighten herself up. "I'm just joking. That felt so good, Papi."

He laughed as he started to regain his breath. "I'm not kicking you out. I just know you have to go. I got what I wanted, so I'm good now."

"Well, I'm glad you are pleased," she said, bending forward and planting a wet kiss on his lips that sent chills through his entire body. "I love you."

"I love you too. I'm so happy you going to be my wife." Steve thought about how much he truly loved her, and his own mind was at war with itself, especially when it was distrusting her. Part of him wanted so bad just to outright ask her if she was going to Jon Jon's funeral, but he decided not to and kept it cool.

Angelia took a few minutes to get herself together before heading out the door.

She jumped in the car and made her way to Esha's place. The entire way, she could feel her pussy throbbing from what Steve had just done to her. She was glad she stuck around to give him some. When she pulled up in Esha's driveway, Esha was sitting in her Range Rover listening to music. "Damn, girl. What the hell was you doing? I told you I was trying to get there early so we could sit closer to the front!" she complained as she gave Angelia a look when she got in the passenger seat.

"My bad, Steve was trying to do it. He was acting all weird and shit, like he thought I was lying about going to a funeral with you."

"Why would you lie about that?"

"I don't know. He was acting weird. I don't know if it was because he had just woke up from a bad dream or what, but he wouldn't let me out the door until I gave him some." Esha put down the sun visor to get the bright sun out of her eyes after making a right hand turn onto the main road.

Esha giggled. "He prolly had a quick flash back of you cheating on him."

They both shook their heads in laughter.

James was three cars behind them, and was on the phone with Steve, updating him on where they were going and giving him all the info along the way. He followed them all the way to Jon Jon's funeral.

"Yea, bro, they just pulled into the parking lot of the funeral home. They going to that nigga's funeral. It's packed to the max over here. They got the streets blocked off and everything. Who the hell was that nigga?"

Steve shook his head. He was crushed. "Why would she go to that nigga's funeral?"

"That's Angelia for you. Little liar. We got her ass now though." He started taking pictures of her and Esha getting out of Esha's Range Rover. He was parked across the street with other cars, so nobody suspected anything. He got a few good pictures of the two of them, so Steve would have more than enough evidence that she couldn't dispute.

Steve was beyond hurt. His stomach was turning and the tone of his voice was starting to change over the phone. "Man, what should I do?"

"What I've been telling you to do! Drop that girl. Leave her alone. Look how many lies you've caught her in. How many more times do you need to catch her? She clearly wants to be doing something else. I hate even seeing you dealing with her because you could have someone that would hold you down way better. I got love for both of you and we been friends for a long time, but Angelia is not the one for you. She a lil' thot."

"Come on, man. Now you being disrespectful." Steve was a little irritated hearing this come out of James' mouth.

"Am I really though? Or am I just speaking the truth? I'm just telling you as a friend, as your brother, you deserve better. I ain't trying to be disrespectful."

Steve shook his head as his eyes started to water. "You right. I just can't believe this. Why wouldn't she just tell me? Like, why lie?"

"Why would she tell you? This the dude you caught her having sex with in y'all house. What the hell would she even say to you? Oh, remember the guy I was fucking in your house . . . yeah, he died so I'ma go pay my respects," James said as he laughed.

"Fuck you." Steve gave the only response he could think of.

"I'm serious though. Bro, she's playing you. You gotta just let her go."

Steve didn't like what he was hearing at all. Normally James would try to keep them together through thick and thin, but now he was telling him that it was better for them to split. At this point, James was over trying to keep them together. He knew what was best for his friend. Angelia had proven again who and what she really was.

The funeral lasted for several hours, and James kept Angelia in his sight from a distance. He continued to get photos. He even followed them to the restaurant everyone went to eat at afterward and got a few of her and Esha going inside. Steve called every 10 or so minutes to get updates on what was happening. Every time he called, it upset him, but he just had to know. James started sending Steve all the pictures from the funeral and each and every one solidified Steve's sadness, and his anger. He had a pit in his stomach, and he needed to think hard about how he planned to approach her about the situation.

CHAPTER
FIFTY-SIX

Esha and Angelia pulled back up into Esha's driveway, and Angelia got right into her car. She sat her purse on the passenger seat and decided to check her phone. Steve had called her 8 times. She backed out of the driveway, and called him as she drove off. He answered on the first ring.

"Damn, I'm glad I wasn't dying."

"Stop it, Steve. I told you I was at a funeral. I had my phone on silent to be respectful. I'm sorry. Are you ok?"

"Yeah, I'm good. I'm good." And then he went silent.

"Hello?"

"Yes, I'm here."

"So you just calling me like that and didn't want anything?"

Steve could hear the hurt in her voice, the sadness from being at a funeral, and that pissed him off even more. He really didn't know what to say. He was speechless. "I'll call you back," was all he could get out.

Angelia hung up, shaking her head while still driving. She cruised along the road wondering what was wrong with Steve. She went to get out her phone, but stopped when two black trucks cut her off and came to a stop in front of her. Two men got out of each truck in black suits with guns drawn and badges in hand. One of them was wearing jeans with a polo shirt and tennis shoes, but still had a badge and gun. Angelia was scared and confused. She put her car in park and threw her hands up in the air.

"Angelia?" the agent asked as he opened the car door with one hand while pointing his gun at her with the other.

"Yes, what's going on?" she asked as the agent took her by the arm and removed her from the vehicle.

"We will tell you in a minute. For now, you need to come with me." He walked her to the back of one of the trucks, opened the door, and helped her get into the back seat. The agent then closed the door and got into the driver's seat. Another agent got into the passenger seat in the front and another one got in the back seat next to her. She looked over her shoulder and saw the one in jeans get into the driver's seat of her car. The trucks began to drive one behind the other one, and her car followed behind them.

"Where all y'all taking me? What's this about?" she asked from the back seat.

"Relax, relax we're just going for a little ride. We just have a few questions to ask you. That's all."

"About what?"

"Jon Jon. Do you know anything about his vicious murder?"

"No, what the hell?"

"You sure? Because we looked through his phone and saw some text messages from you to him. It looked like you were pretty mad at him, since he robbed you and your boyfriend."

Angelia's heart dropped. She was now terrified and her hands were shaking.

"Didn't know we knew that, huh?" he added as the agent in the front and the agent next to her started laughing. "We also know that you're the one that crashed your piece of shit car into his hundred thousand dollar BMW that night. Then you reported your car stolen as if you didn't do it." The other agents continued to laugh. It was like they were having fun with all of this.

"I don't know what you are talking about. Let me out of here, please. I have to go."

"Calm down. Tell us who you think killed Jon Jon."

"I have no clue. I'm sorry I'm not able to help you." Tears started rolling down Angelia's cheeks.

"Ok, you can't help with that one, but let's see if you can help us with this one. Where was he getting all of his drugs? Who was his supplier?"

"I have no clue."

"Your dad?" the agent in the passenger seat turned around and asked with a smile. Angelia didn't like where this was going. She didn't like anything about what was happening.

"I don't know anything!" she yelled in anger. "Let me out of this truck right now!"

CHAPTER
FIFTY-SEVEN

he agent driving pulled over while still laughing. He got out and opened her door. "We'll be seeing you soon, Angelia," the agent who was driving her car said as he handed her her car keys. She took her car keys, ran to her car, and slammed the door. Her heart was beating so fast and she was shaking so bad she couldn't drive. She took deep breaths trying to calm herself down. She had no idea what to do, who to call, or where to go. It was obvious that the Feds were all over this murder.

James had been behind them the whole time on the phone with Steve.

"They just let her go?"

"Yeah, they just hit some blocks and gave her back her car. I don't know what the fuck that was, bro. You better watch her, bro. I'm telling you, she may be plotting to take you down or something. I'm going to come talk to you in person later. That shit got me over here paranoid."

"You sure it was the Feds?"

"Yes, nigga! I'm over here watching all this shit in 3D, bro. It was definitely the Feds!"

"I'm about to call her," Steve said before he hung up the phone and called Angelia.

"Hello," she answered.

"What you doing?"

"Driving home. You need anything before I get there?"

"Naw, naw, I'm good. Um, I'll be there when you get there. How was the funeral?"

"Very sad, but it was beautiful."

"Are you ok?"

"Yeah, I'm fine."

"Ok, good. I'll see you shortly then."

"Ok, Papi."

Angelia hung up and her mind was racing. She was terrified. She didn't know what was going through Steve's mind. She was regretting ever going to Jon Jon's funeral or even dealing with him before hand. She knew that the Feds didn't play games, and that they would do any and everything necessary to get what they wanted. She could feel herself buckling under the stress. She wanted to tell Steve, but didn't know where to even begin. She had to come up with something to say because she wanted to at least warn him that the Feds were on her, and the heat could possibly spill over into his world. Angelia pulled up into the driveway, and took a deep breath. She was shaking, but she had to go inside. Her mind continued to race about what she would say. She still wasn't sure when she opened the side door and went in. Before the door closed behind her, Steve slapped the spit out of her mouth. "Lying ass bitch! You went to Jon Jon's funeral!"

Angelia was caught off guard and dropped straight to the floor holding her face. He had never hit her like that, and she was more shocked than she was in pain.

"I didn't! What is wrong with you?" she said as she got up off the floor.

"Don't lie to me!"

"I'm not lying. I didn't go. You got issues!" she responded, pushing him in the shoulder and making her way past him.

"Angelia," Steve said calmly and softly. The tone of his voice stopped her in her tracks and she turned around. Steve was holding his phone. "I have something I need to show you. Come here."

Angelia reluctantly walked back toward him and stood beside him. Steve pulled up the first picture of her and Esha getting out of Esha's truck at the funeral. "Bitch! I got you on camera!" Steve screamed as he swiped through photo after photo. Angelia just covered her mouth in shock.

After the third or fourth picture, she could feel a rage welling up within her. "Wow! You really don't trust me. You had someone follow me and take pictures? Fuck you, Steve!" she shouted as she ran up the staircase.

Steve yelled behind her, "What? You got nothing to say? I caught your ass and you can't say shit." He started to climb up the stairs to continue the argument when the first armful of his clothes hit him in the head.

"Get out of here!" Angelia screamed as she threw his stuff down the stairs at him. "You a fucking insecure little ass boy that have to hire someone to follow me because you insecure as fuck. Fuck you! I'm done with this amateur shit!" she yelled as she threw handful after handful of his stuff.

Steve was confused as to why she seemed to be more mad than he was. He was speechless as she continued to throw his things down the stairs. He stood at the top of the stairs in silence, just watching her for a few minutes and then he said, "Why would you go to that nigga's funeral?"

Angelia paused with another handful of his stuff in her arms, looked at him, and calmly said, "I didn't." Then she threw the stuff down the stairs.

How can she deny it again when I just showed her the pictures? This girl is a fucking mess, Steve thought. He felt himself getting angry again and his heart started pounding, so he stormed out of the house rather than make a bad decision. He called James to let him know he was on his way over. Steve backed out of his driveway fast, running over a piece of the lawn. He skidded his tires as he took off in a rage. He punched his steering wheel a few times while driving down the road. The sun was starting to set, giving off a pinkish, purplish glow off in the horizon. Steve drove fast, but in complete silence. He saw a liquor store on the right and turned off the street quickly, parking his car by the front door instead of in a parking spot. He marched into the liquor store.

The Chaldean store owner greeted him pleasantly, "What can I get you today, bro?"

Steve was in no mood for small talk. "Remy. A fifth," he said as he set a hundred dollar bill on the table. The owner grabbed the liquor and set it on the counter. Steve grabbed it and walked out the door, not waiting for a bag or his change. He got in his car and threw it in reverse, backing recklessly out into the street and tearing off with his gas pedal to the floor. He drove with his knees as he opened up the bottle. He started taking big gulps out of the bottle, getting the majority of the bottle down in about a minute. By the time he got to James' house, the liquor was taking effect.

CHAPTER
FIFTY-EIGHT

J ames glanced at Steve as he came through the door with the bottle of Remy in his hand. He had a blunt hanging out of his mouth, and was playing Madden. Steve thought about how his life could be more peaceful like James' if he didn't have a girl like Angelia ruining it all the time. Steve dropped backwards into the couch, and slid forward, almost falling off. He threw his finger in the air, and drunkenly mumbled, "That fucking bitch . . . " and James just shook his head.

"Man, you need to stop drinking like that. That ain't the right way to handle your stress. She's not even worth it, bro," James said as he paused the game to give Steve his full attention.

"I don't even care. She don't love me, bro. There's no way she loves me," Steve said as he opened up the bottle and took another drink.

"She probably does love you, but wants other things in her life too."

Steve tilted up the bottle again and squinted his face because the drink didn't go down as smoothly this time. "I don't give a fuck about nothing, bro. Life is fucked up. Just look at this shit. Look what I'm going through with all this money, bro. This money shit is overrated. I thought my problems were supposed to go away, not grow once I got money! Why is this bitch like this, bro? I'ma kill her. I want to kill her right now, for real." By the time he finished, James had walked over to him, and grabbed the bottle out of his hand and put the cap on. Steve reached out for the bottle, but wasn't going to get up or put any real effort into getting it back.

"Man you are good. You don't need to kill her. You just have to get her out of your life, for real. She is a bad energy that you don't need. You've made it to a level that most guys in your lane will never get to. You are definitely blessed, but it's time for you to start weeding out the bad energy."

Steve shook his head as he listened. He sat back up and rested his head in his hands. "Why do I love her so much? Fuck!" he shouted, feeling like throwing his fist through a wall.

"It's alright to love someone, but you can't let somebody drag you down. I'm sick of watching her stress you out like this. You're making all the right moves while she makes the wrong ones. She needs to go, for sure. I don't really know what it's going to take for you to let her go. I got this bad feeling that if you stay with her, she's going to have you in some deep shit. Just like how the Feds ran down on her like that. Nigga, she's into something that you don't need no part of with the business you are in."

"I need to say something to her about that. That's some weird shit."

"Say something for what? She's just going to lie about that too. You need to leave that girl. She's not right for you at all. Maybe you need to hear it from your Uncle Swift or something. Imagine what Swift would say if you told him she got picked up and dropped back off by the Feds. Come on, Steve! You gotta think. All the signs are there. You caught her fucking in your house, then she lied about going to the same dude's funeral. Plus, she's fucking other niggas in the hood behind your back. Nigga, you a boss now. You need to strap on your nuts and get a way better chick and leave her where she's at, which is nowhere."

Steve nodded his head, but still didn't want to accept what was absolutely clear to everyone except him. "I need to think. I'm about to get me a suite and lay back. I have to think, bro. This shit crazy. I'm telling you, bro, life ain't supposed to be like this. I don't do shit to deserve this. For my wife to treat me like this after all I do for her . . . that's not cool. I do everything for that girl and she out looking elsewhere like I ain't shit. I gotta lay back, bro. I'll catch up with you later, bro." Steve's eyes began to water and one tear fell to the ground as he walked out the door.

James didn't want his friend to drive drunk like that, but he also knew that there was nothing he could tell him that would stop him, so he just let him leave. James opened the door and yelled out, "Call me once you make it to your destination. You've been drinking and shit." James shook his head. "Oh yeah, leave that gun here too, bro."

Steve turned around and handed the gun to James and left. Steve took off on the road more cautiously this time. He was drunk, and didn't want to get pulled over for something stupid. By this time, the sun had set completely and the night time air was cool. He cracked his windows and let the air rush through the car as he drove again in silence. He knew of a five start hotel that was only a few miles down the road, so he decided he would go there. *First, though, I gotta get myself something to drink*, Steve thought. He stopped at another liquor store and got another bottle of Remy. This time, he waited for his change and for the employee to put it in a bag. A couple minutes later, he arrived at the hotel. He walked right inside and told the lady at the desk to give him the best room they had. She proceeded to check what all was available in the computer, then asked for a credit card.

You've gotta be kidding me, Steve thought to himself. He only had a wad of cash on him. "I'll be back in a minute," Steve said as he walked out the front door calling James. James said he would bring him up a card and put the room in his name. Either way, this was still one more inconvenience for Steve that just irritated him more. He had all this money, yet he still had to rely on other people. Steve waited in his car for James to get there. It only took him about 5 minutes to arrive, and James walked right in and got the room. When he came back out to Steve's car, James got in for a second and looked over at him. "Bro, you're gonna be fine. You don't need that girl. Lay back and enjoy yourself tonight and don't think too much." James handed him the room key, patted him on the shoulder, and left.

CHAPTER
FIFTY-NINE

W hen Steve got to his room, it was beautiful, but he didn't pay much attention to how nice it really was. Nothing could make him happy at the moment. He sat down at the end of the king size bed and cried. Steve looked over at the wet bar located at the other end of the suite. It had nice, crystal rocks glasses sitting on the top along with a set of stainless steel tongs. He got up and made his way over there, grabbing one of the glasses, and filling it with ice. He poured the Remy over ice and took a sip.

I could use a little water with my Remy, he thought to himself and let out a little laugh. He kicked his feet up on the bed, and leaned back against the headboard. He thought about how crazy life was at the moment, but he didn't know what to do about that except to take another sip of his drink and put his phone on silent. He sat his phone on the bed next to him, and continued to take sips of his drink. The ice made a clinking sound in the bottom of his glass as he finished off the Remy. He got up, and waddled his way back over to the wet bar where he had set his bottle down.

He sloppily got himself a few more cubes of ice, and filled his glass up almost all the way to the top. He tried to be as careful as possible to not spill his drink on the way back to the bed, but he was beyond tipsy at this point. A few splashes hit the floor before he set the glass down on the nightstand. He sat back on the bed again. Silence. He took a look at his phone and picked it up. He called Angelia, and she sent him straight to voicemail after a half of one ring. He could feel himself getting upset again, and he called back. She sent him to voicemail again, so he left her a message. He then continued to call and leave her message after message.

"I can't believe you, bitch!" he slurred. "You think this shit funny? Stupid bitch, pick up the phone since you want to lie. Pick up the fucking phone! Bitch! Why you not answering my calls? You think I don't love you or something? Naw, you don't love me do you? You can't love me, because you just step all over me. I know you don't love me." Steve continued talking until the time for the message ran out, then he took another drink and did it again.

"You know what? You not even worth it. I don't even know why I'm tripping. You just a hoe! That's all. And I don't need to be with a hoe. What's the point of that?" He hung up the phone, and kept drinking. A few seconds later he picked up the phone again.

"Please answer the phone and explain to me why you treat me like this. I'm just curious. I'm not coming home tonight, but I love you and I'm somewhere safe. Love you." He hung up and dropped his phone on the bed next to him. The liquor took some of the pain away, but he was still hurt and felt like he was going crazy. He took another sip of his drink, and went to set it back on the nightstand, but it dropped on the floor, spilling all over the carpet. Steve glanced down at the floor, and swung his legs off the bed, putting his feet on the floor. He left the drink there, and walked into the bathroom to take a piss. He stood there swaying back and forth, trying to center his urine stream with more than a little difficulty. He flushed the toilet and walked past the wet bar, grabbing his bottle, and taking it back to the bed with him. He wondered what Angelia was doing, where she was, and why she wasn't answering. He opened the bottle and tilted it back, taking a big pull that sent goosebumps throughout his body. He called Angelia again and got her voicemail. He tried to sound a little less crazy this time.

"Hey, just calling to make sure you was ok. Call me back, please. I'm getting worried about you." He hung up the phone and called James.

CHAPTER
SIXTY

"What's up? You good?" James answered.

"Yeah, I'm good. I need you to drive by the house and see if Ang is there."

James could tell by the sound of Steve's voice that he was wasted. "Bro, why don't you just look on your phone and check the cameras. You can see outside and inside the house from right where you're at. All that shit is hooked up in there."

"Ohhhhh, right, right. Ok, let me see something . . . I'll call you back," Steve said, hanging up the phone and opening up his camera app.

He looked on the living room camera and could see Angelia sitting there talking on the phone. "Aha! I see you there," he said, closing the app and calling her again.

She sent him straight to voicemail.

"You might as well answer. I see you sitting right there on the couch in the living room talking on the phone. Did you forget I got cameras all over the house? Pick up the phone!" he yelled and switched back to the camera app. She was still sitting there doing the same thing, so he called her again.

"Come on, Angelia! Stop playing and answer the damn phone. Like what the fuck is wrong with you? You clearly don't really love me I see. You over there acting like you don't want to talk to me. Just answer the phone for two minutes. I can see you sitting right on the couch. You probably on the phone with your other nigga." He hung up the phone and went to check his cameras again. The one that showed where she was sitting was completely black, along with three other ones. He couldn't tell if they were covered, or ripped off the wall or what. He could feel the alcohol fueled anger building up in him again as he called James.

"Hey, call the camera company and tell them the cameras ain't working!"

"What you mean?"

"I was just looking at Angelia in the crib and the cameras went black."

James could tell Steve was even more drunk than he was before. He wanted to laugh, but instead he said, "Have you talked to her?"

"Naw, not yet. Left a couple voicemails. You know how I do," he slurred.

"Oh, she didn't answer."

"Naw, she acting crazy. I called her and told her I could see her ass sitting on the couch. She was literally sitting on the couch having a full blown conversation with someone while ignoring the shit outta me. She didn't pick up one of my calls!"

James shook his head. "Give her some time. She probably just doesn't want to talk to you right now. I'll call and see what's up with the cameras not working," he lied, knowing that there was nothing wrong with the cameras and that Angelia just disconnected them.

"Ok, let me know what they say. I'm chillin'. I ain't tripping over that bitch. If she really loved me, she wouldn't be playing me like this. We both know I deserve way better than her ass. Who the fuck is her? You feel me? Bitch, you ain't even got a job. You broke. You feel me, bro?"

"Yeah, bro. I feel you."

"All the shit I did for her, and you do me like this?" Steve kept going on and on. James had been incredibly patient, but he was getting tired of listening to it now. By this point, Steve was wasted and talking out of the side of his neck. James knew that after a good night's sleep, Steve would be back to normal tomorrow, even if he was a little hungover. Steve continued to ramble for another hour about how much better off he was without Angelia and how he didn't deserve the shit she put him through. James knew, though, that he'd be back in his feelings tomorrow. After Steve hung up the phone, Steve took another swig off his bottle, laid on his side, and cried himself to sleep.

CHAPTER
SIXTY-ONE

Steve opened up one of his eyes as the sun beamed through the window on his face. It was 8 in the morning, and Steve let out a groan. He had a massive headache. He laid there for a minute to try and get the motivation to get up. Eventually, he swung his legs off the side of the bed, and sat up. He was spinning and his mouth started to water. He ran to the bathroom and started dry heaving into the toilet. *Fuck, I should've had something to eat yesterday*, he thought as he hugged the toilet while on his knees. The thought of food made him start dry heaving again and he vomited a thin, yellow, acidic liquid into the toilet. He laid himself down on the cold tile floor, trying to get his mind together. After laying there for an hour feeling sorry for himself, he ordered some room service. They brought biscuits and gravy to his room, and he devoured it. He turned on the shower and stood in there for an hour. While he was in the shower, he thought about what he needed to do. *I'ma go see Uncle Swift, and see what he has to say. He'll have some good advice for me*, he thought.

When he got out of the shower, he had calls from his cousins, Kane, Juice, and several other people, but he didn't feel like dealing with anything today, so he just ignored them. The only name he wanted to see on his caller ID was Angelia, and it wasn't there.

As Steve stepped out of the hotel into the morning air, he heard the sound of lawnmowers and leaf blowers and smelled the fresh cut grass. After getting out from under the entryway, the sunlight hit him in the face, reminding him of his headache that still hadn't quite went away. He got in his car and made the trip to Milan to see his uncle.

Swift had a huge smile on his face as Steve came walking up, until he got close. Swift could see the hurt and pain in his face. He could tell something wasn't right. "What happened, Nephew?" he asked with open arms.

Steve hugged him and shook his head. "It's all bad . . . It's all bad."

Swift wasn't sure what he meant, but sat down quickly across from Steve to see what was going on. "What's the matter?"

"I don't even know where to start. Life has been crazy for me. Angelia is a bitch, man."

"What she do?"

"A lot . . . she did a lot. First, I catch her having sex with a guy at our house. Then, I get robbed for some bricks. I had no idea who did it, but later found out that it was the guy she was having sex with at the house."

"She set that up?"

"No, I don't believe that."

"Of course you don't. Where was you keeping it at?"

"At a whole different house that only a few people knew about."

"Did she know?"

"Yeah, but she didn't have anything to do with it."

"How can you be so sure? You think that kinda shit just happens out of the blue?" Swift tossed his arms up in the air to emphasize his point.

"No, but . . . "

"But nothing. It sounds like she set you up, nephew. End of story."

"She wouldn't do that, Unk. It wasn't her. For sure it wasn't. I don't know how it happened, but it wasn't her. I put it on my life."

Swift took in a deep breath, and figured his nephew wasn't telling him every single detail. He was clearly holding something back. "So, he took the stuff?"

"Yeah, and now he's dead."

"Good. He should be."

"His funeral was yesterday, and Angelia lied to me and went," Steve said as he looked at the floor, shuffling his feet, knowing how ridiculous it probably sounded to Swift that he was defending her at this point.

"She went to his funeral?" Uncle Swift asked, leaning forward with wide open eyes.

"Yeah. We supposed to get married and everything and she went to his funeral."

Swift shook his head. "How much do you owe?"

"Oh, no. That's covered, Unk. I already took care of that. I'm in the green with Karo. We are good there, no worries. Karo's the one who actually made him disappear."

"Not surprised. How did she know?"

"That's a good question. I can't even tell you."

CHAPTER
SIXTY-TWO

Uncle Swift let out a big sigh, and slid down into his chair. He thought his nephew was a lot smarter than this. "This girl got you going crazy."

"She don't, Unk. I'm focused for sure." Steve nodded his head, hoping his uncle would believe him.

Swift raised his voice. "She's the reason for all this bullshit!" He took a deep breath and lowered his voice and continued, "Not one thing you have told me didn't have her playing a part in it. She's dragging you down and you are going to whine up dead or in prison for a very long time if you keep dealing with her. With that said, I'm cutting you and Karo's relationship off until you get rid of this girl. We have no room for mistakes like that. So, pay her what you owe, and she's going to back off."

"Unk, you not even giving me a chance to clean this up."

"I gave you a chance, and you about to fuck it up. This girl Angelia got you wrapped up, and you are missing way too many important signs. You just ignoring shit like this is some kind of game. You're done. Pay her what you owe her, and it's over. Whatever money or bricks you have left . . . start a new life. This ain't the life for you at all. If you going to continue to be weak for these stupid ass little girls, this is not going to work for you."

"Unk, come on, man."

"It's over." Swift was pissed and he hoped that Steve hadn't created more damage than he was willing to admit to him. He was disappointed in Steve, and even more disappointed that he couldn't see what was a clear and present danger right in front of his eyes. He was unwilling to wake up and make the hard choices to keep going, so this is what it had to come to. He also smelled the liquor from the night before on Steve's breath, and saw the heavy bags under his eyes. "You need to pull yourself together, and figure out what you really want to do with your life. You definitely need to leave this crazy ass girl alone no matter what you decide. She ain't nothing but bad news."

"Can you have a talk with her?"

Swift's eyes lit up in anger. Steve still didn't get it. "For what? What else do you want her to do to you?"

"Just find out where her mind is at and if she really loves me."

Uncle Swift shook his head and threw his hands up in the air. He didn't understand his nephew at all. Steve was serious, and he could tell he cared about this girl. He clearly didn't care about the money, the drugs, or the new relationship he had built with Karo. Angelia was more important to him than all that, and in Swift's eyes, she was going to be his downfall. "I really can't believe this shit," Swift finally said.

"What? You're acting like I'm not human. I'm not into what you and my dad were into. I only want and care about one woman. I don't need multiple women. What's wrong with that?" Steve started to tear up.

"It's nothing wrong with it, nephew." Swift couldn't relate at all to what he was feeling, but he wasn't going to just overlook the very real pain he could see in his nephew either. "Just get yourself together. I don't want to see you get in trouble or have to go through more pain and suffering because of a girl. It's ok to be in love, nephew. But, it's not ok to let it ruin your life, and that's what's happening." Swift looked at Steve for a few minutes. He looked pathetic, just sitting there with his head down and tears running from his eyes. *All because of a girl that don't even treat him right,* Swift thought. He started to feel compassion for his nephew, so he reached out and hugged him, holding him in his arms. Tears continued to fall from Steve's eyes as he rested his head on his uncle's shoulder. Steve was hurt and heartbroken. He knew he needed to get a grip on things, but he didn't know where to even start. He was embarrassed, but couldn't help it. His emotions had overpowered everything, and he still loved Angelia for some reason.

"I'll talk to her if you want . . . no problem," uncle Swift said, releasing his hug and patting Steve on the shoulder.

"Thanks," Steve said with a forced smile. "I just need to know." Steve wiped the tears away from his eyes with his forearm and asked, "So what am I going to do now?"

"It's time to get your mind right. Iron out everything with that girl."

"What should I do about her going to the funeral?"

"Just forgive her. You clearly don't want to leave her, so what's the point of causing confusion. Just address it with her. Let her know that all she has to do is be honest with you and y'all will be good."

Steve understood what his uncle was saying, and his uncle was right. He loved her so much and it didn't make sense to push her away because all he would do is hurt himself by doing that. Talking with his uncle made him feel much better. After thanking him for his wisdom, Steve said goodbye to Swift and went out into the prison's parking lot. He sat in the car for a moment and thought. He then grabbed his phone out and sent Angelia an apology text. Although he was losing his plug, all he wanted was Angelia. She never responded to his message, but she 'Loved' it after a few seconds, which made him feel good. As he drove out of the prison, he started returning all the phone calls he had missed from earlier. He called James to tell him that he was going to stop by. He turned up his music, and rolled down his windows. The hangover was still there, but mentally, he was feeling great about everything. About 20 minutes later, he pulled up in James' driveway. He couldn't wait to go inside and tell him about everything.

CHAPTER
SIXTY-THREE

J ames listened patiently to everything Steve had to say. He didn't agree with a lot of what Steve was saying, but he decided he was going to just be supportive, so he nodded his head and tried to be encouraging.

"Man, I just love her," Steve said as he was sitting down at the kitchen table across from James.

"I see. If that's what makes you happy, bro, go for it. Forgive and forget, because I never want to see you how you were yesterday. That was crazy."

Steve laughed. "My uncle always knows how to pull me back together fast. He's like my counselor. I want him to talk to Angelia and see if he can get through to her."

"That would be good. I'm hoping he can get through to her because I didn't know what to do to help you. You was tripping. So uncle Swift said he'd talk to her?"

Steve laughed. "She gets to me so bad. And yeah, he said he will have a talk with her," Steve said, nodding his head, hoping that a talk with Swift would really help like he wanted it to.

"So you good now?"

"I feel better. I sent her a text saying I apologize and all that and I want her to know she can tell me anything no matter what. I told her I wasn't mad about the funeral and I don't want to beef about it. She 'Loved' the message, so hopefully shit cool. At least it should be . . . I don't know. I'll go to the crib later on. I'ma chill with you today. I need to be around positive energy. I'll help you water some plants and shit if you need help.

"I can always use a hand with that for sure," James told him. "Matter of fact, the lights come on in my flowering room in about an hour, so I'ma whoop your ass in Madden right quick, and then we can go down and get some work done. Cool?" James gave him a pound.

"Cool," Steve said with a smile.

"$100?" James asked.

"Naw, $500, and I'ma whoop yo' ass."

"Bet."

They sat down and played a game of Madden. James absolutely devastated him in the game. He got up and was screaming in Steve's face, making sure he knew that he was the king of Madden. Steve reached in his pocket and took out five $100 bills and handed them over.

"Thank you!" James said with a big grin. "Let's head downstairs now. The lights been on about 5 minutes."

They made their way to the basement, and first took a look into the veg room. All the plants were looking deep green and lush under the cool white lights. Oscillating fans moved back and forth, sending a breeze across the canopy.

"Damn, you really doing this shit!" Steve said, impressed with the progress.

"Yeah, they looking good. I had some spotting on my leaves about two weeks ago. The book I have had a picture of a leaf in it that looked like mine, and it said it could be a calcium deficiency. I added an extra teaspoon of CalMag into my vegetative nutrient mix, the spotting went away a few days later, and everything looks good now."

"CalMag? What is that?"

"Oh, that's calcium and magnesium. People call it CalMag for short. Plants need both of those nutrients to grow properly, and some strains need more of them than others."

Steve nodded his head as James explained some of the different strains he was working with now, and some of the techniques he was trying. "But this ain't nothing. It's time to move over to the flowering room."

CHAPTER
SIXTY-FOUR

Steve followed James out of the veg room and they walked a few feet over to the newly built flowering room. James opened the door and Steve stepped inside. He was immediately smacked in the face with an almost indescribable skunky, garlicy, rotten fruit smell. "These plants over here will be coming down in about a week," James began, as he put on a pair of black nitrile gloves to handle some of the plants. "They've been getting straight water for a few days now, and will continue to get nothing put pure H2O until they come down." James pulled out his phone and plugged in what looked like a little camera to it. He called Steve over as he put the camera up close to one of the buds. A close up image showed up on his phone. "See, look here. Those things that look like mushrooms all over the buds are called trichomes. See how the heads on the 'mushrooms' look clear right now?"

"Yeah. They do look clear. That camera is like a little ass microscope."

James laughed. "Over the coming days, the heads of those trichomes will turn milky, and then some will start to turn amber. I watch those trichomes for the perfect time to harvest." Steve was amazed at what he was seeing. James called him over to the other side of the room. "These plants are about two weeks into flowering. They will finish up at about 9 weeks. See how they have buds starting to form all over them? See all those white hairs? Those are pistils, part of the flower of a female plant."

"That shit is crazy," Steve said as they closed the door behind them. "So, what do you need me to do?"

"See those two large, blue barrels over there? Those are 55 gallons a piece. We will need both of those to water the flowering room. The plants that are almost done are getting plain water, and I'll show you how to mix up the flowering nutrients for the others. You can start by filling that barrel on the left with plain reverse osmosis water." Steve walked over to the barrel, and James plugged in a submersible pump and handed Steve a hose. "After that barrel is filled, fill the other one, then we will mix up the nutes," James instructed him. After about 20 minutes, all the watering was done and they were back upstairs.

Steve felt good helping out his friend. The time flew, and it kept his mind off things. On his way home, Steve stopped at the liquor store and picked up a big bottle of Angelia and his favorite liquor. As Steve pulled into the driveway, he noticed that the house looked pretty dark inside. Everything was quiet. He came inside and set the bottle of liquor on the counter and flipped on the kitchen lights. "Angelia?" No response, just silence. He walked up the stairs and into the bedroom where he found Angelia asleep on her side, with a half empty glass of liquor sitting on the nightstand beside her. The radio was playing low. Steve smiled, wondering if she had been feeling as bad as he had. Since he had been out and about all day, he took his clothes off, and jumped in the shower. He was so happy to be back home, and he was happy that his girl was right there outside the bathroom door, laying in bed. After his shower, he put on some lotion and Angelia's favorite cologne. He ran back downstairs, and took two quick shots of liquor back to back, then ran up the stairs and crawled in bed next to her. She was tucked under the comforter, but when he lifted it up to get under it, he noticed she was butt naked. He got closer, putting his arm around her, and kissing the back of her shoulder. He felt so good being next to her, and she smelled so good to him. "I love you," he whispered.

CHAPTER
SIXTY-FIVE

S
he slowly turned her head around and looked at him. "I love you too," she whispered back. She started kissing him softly and passionately. They tongue wrestled for a few minutes, putting their hands all over each other. Electric shocks were traveling through both of their bodies as they couldn't get enough of each other.

"I'm sorry, baby," he whispered as he got on top of her and began kissing her breasts. He made his way down to her stomach, then traced his tongue down to her moist pussy. He licked up the juices that were between her pussy lips, then made his way up to her clit. He started sucking on it, and Angelia let out a few moans.

"Yes, Papi," she moaned as she spread her legs apart, and put her hands on the back of his head. Steve was licking all over her pussy. He threw her legs back, and even started licking her asshole. "Yes, Papi. It feels so good when you lick my ass like that," she said in a low, sexy tone.

He continued to hold her legs back, licking all over her ass. He then started spitting in it, then sucking his spit up. He started to stick his tongue in and out of her ass while he plunged his index finger in her pussy. He moved his mouth up to her clit, and started licking and sucking it while he slid his finger in her ass.

"Papi, I'm going to cum," she moaned, massaging her tits and feeling herself about to explode. Steve continued to lick and lick while fingering her asshole until her pussy started creaming. "I'm cumming, Papi! Shittt!" she moaned as if it took everything she had to push the cream out of her pussy. Her toes curled as she orgasmed, then she felt her body go limp and she gasped for air. "Papi, put your dick in me. I'm so wet."

Steve took off his boxer briefs and put his already rock hard dick right inside her wetness, and started stroking her to the R&B song that was playing on the radio.

After about twelve pumps he was cumming and didn't want to prolong it anymore. He released everything he had inside her. "Damn, Papi. Why did you cum?" she asked as he rolled off her.

"I couldn't hold it. My bad," he replied as he lay on his back, breathing heavily.

"We gotta get it back up," she said, getting on top of him and starting to suck his dick. She worked at it, but it kept getting softer and softer.

"Give me a sec, boo."

"Okay," she said as she stopped trying and laid down next to him. "What you drinking? I want some."

"It's plenty over there." Steve pointed to the bottle he brought up with him that was sitting on the nightstand.

Angelia hopped up and took a drink out of the bottle. She handed it to Steve. "Here, your turn," she said after swallowing her big gulp. He took a big drink off the bottle and shivered a little, then gave her a big smile. She was looking so good to him sitting there naked with a messy bun piled up on top of her head. He looked at her with loving eyes, just taking in the moment.

Angelia sat the bottle of liquor back down on the nightstand on her side of the bed and opened up the drawer. She pulled out a small bag of cocaine and gave it a little shake while smiling. Steve was wondering what she was doing, but just sat there watching her. She poured out a pile on the dresser, and scraped it into a line with a credit card. She then rolled up a hundred dollar bill, and sniffed it. She pinched her nose for a second, then gave Steve a smile. He was surprised that she did coke. He had never seen her do it before. He, himself had never even tried it. "You playing, right?" he said as he tilted his head at her, giving her a confused look.

"No, Papi. Come on. Just do one line with me. It's going to make your dick hard again too."

Steve sat there watching her as she poured out another small pile, and lined it up. He took a deep breath and asked, "What do I do, just suck it up my nose?"

"Yeah, here," she said, handing him the rolled up bill.

Steve took the bill, put it in one nostril, plugged his other one like he saw her do, and started sniffing up the small line of coke. He wasn't exactly the most graceful, but he got it all up. "Shit," he said as he looked at her with wide eyes. He then squinted his eyes and face up and shook his head.

"Ok, drink this again. This going to level it out," she told him. He did as he was instructed. After taking another big drink, he laid back down on the bed. He could feel the cocaine coursing through his body. His heartrate increased and he felt a rush of pleasure come over his body. His vision was slightly blurred, and Angelia looked like three different chicks. He didn't know what to say or do. He was stuck, and Angelia took full advantage of him in this condition, riding his hard dick, while making herself cum multiple times. She rode his dick forward, backward, sideways, and in a splits position. Steve was completely out of it. For being his first time doing cocaine, even though the line was small, the purity was so good that it completely rocked his world. He was completely numb except for when he felt himself cumming inside her. The coke enhanced the sensation of him cumming so much more that he started yelling and jerking his body as he came. He loved it.

After cumming, his dick was still standing tall, and Angelia was riding it while cum dripped out of her pussy, down his shaft, and onto the bed. "Who's dick is this, Papi?" she moaned as she started to ride him nice and slow, moving forward and backward with him deep inside of her. He was out of it, and barely heard what she said. "Papi, can you hear me?" she asked as she kept riding him. He just laid there, staring at the ceiling. She grabbed him by the face, and tongue kissed him, shocking him back to reality. "There you go. Who's dick is this, Papi?"

"Your dick, baby. This your dick, baby."

"Forever?" she asked, still working her hips. She was soaking wet.

"Forever and ever, baby," he said, slurring his words.

The sensation of being inside her felt so good to him, but he still felt stuck. Luckily, Angelia stayed on top of him, taking full control. He continued to simply lay back, and enjoy the feelings she was giving him and the cocaine high.

Angelia continued to make herself cum over and over again until she fell asleep on top of his dick, still hard inside of her. The coke had his dick hard as a rock, even in his sleep. It had affected him like a Viagra pill, and Angelia loved every moment of it.

CHAPTER
SIXTY-SIX

When Angelia woke up the following morning, she looked over at Steve laying there, sleeping peacefully. She pulled back the covers and saw that his dick was still hard as a rock as he laid there on his back. She decided to take full advantage of it, and started to ride him. After about a minute, Steve started to wake up and she continued to ride him until he came, moments after she did.

"Good morning, Papi," she said as she climbed off of him, his nut leaking out of her.

"Good morning, baby. Damn, I don't even remember falling asleep. That shit had me twisted."

She giggled. "Did you have fun though?"

"Hell yeah, I did."

They both laughed.

"I did too. That dick was so good. I couldn't get enough. I love it when it's rock hard like that, ouu Papi," she said while shaking him playfully.

He laughed.

"Imagine if I was fucking you with that rock hard ass dick."

"I'd be squirting all over the place," she said with wide eyes and a smile.

He laughed and sat up. He got up, and started getting dressed.

"Where you going, Papi? You acting like you in a rush to get somewhere."

"I have to run some errands. Gotta pick up some money and shit."

"Then come back here? Let's lay up, party, and fuck all day today. Let me get you twisted again. You won't even have to get out of bed. I'll take care of you all day. Today is makeup/baby making day for us."

He laughed. "Ok, I'ma take you up on that."

"So I'ma leave these curtains closed all day to keep the light out of here. I'm going to change the sheets, make food, pour drinks, set out the coke, and get everything ready for when you come back. Then after you done handling all your business, you can come home and let me take care of you."

Steve was smiling as he splashed water on his face in the bathroom. He brushed his teeth, sprayed some cologne on, and grabbed a t-shirt. He was liking what she was saying and was looking forward to getting back and chilling with her for the rest of the day while she catered to him. As he finished getting ready, his mind started to wander a little. He was a little concerned about the whole coke thing. He wondered how long she had been doing it for. She all of the sudden seemed very comfortable showing him that she was doing it. He wasn't necessarily judging her. He was just curious. He shook his head to get the wandering thoughts away, and started to focus on the remainder of the day. He was looking forward to seeing how fucked up they could get together.

They always had fun drinking together, so he couldn't wait to see what the coke would add into the mix.

"Ok, baby. I'll be back soon. Where are your keys? I'ma take your car and make these drop offs."

Angelia's heart all the sudden dropped as she had a flashback of the Feds running up on her, and how they may have a bug inside her car or even a tracker. "Naw, Papi, take yours. I may have to run out for a sec."

"Okay, that's cool. See you in a little bit." Steve paused. "Wait, I have a question for you."

"What's that?"

"How long you been doing coke and how much you be doing?"

She giggled. "I am not a coke head if that's what you're thinking. I been doing it for about a year. And I only do like one or two lines. I don't go further than that. And I'll say I probably do it about three times a month."

"Oh, ok. Good. I was about to say."

She giggled. "No, it's not like that at all."

Steve walked up to her and gave her a kiss while putting his hands on the side of her face. "Ok, baby. I just never want to have to worry about you. I'ma go take care of this shit and then I'm all yours." She smiled at him and he made his way to the basement.

While he was in the basement, Steve gathered up 20 kilos for Juice. He tossed them into a duffle bag, then stashed them in his car. As Steve pulled out of the garage, everything seemed gray. A light rain was coming down that felt more like a mist than a real rain. While he was on the way to see Juice, his mind wandered all over the place. He had a lot to do, and a lot of decisions to make, but all he really wanted to do was get back to the house to chill with Angelia. Juice had been working his way up, moving more and more. Steve was getting ready to start giving him half of everything he bought, that way they could see each other less and make fewer, but larger transactions.

Steve's mind wandered back to Angelia. He was thinking about what James said about Angelia being pulled over. He thought about everything his uncle had talked to him about. He had to figure out what was going on with her, and exactly what happened when she got stopped like that. For now though, he wanted to just clear his head and focus on being peaceful with her.

CHAPTER
SIXTY-SEVEN

After making the drop to Juice, Steve stopped back at the crib to pick up some more kilos for the twins and a few for some other people that had been waiting on him. The twins were now getting 10 kilos at a time, and were moving them pretty quickly. Although for the last few days, the stress had really been eating at Steve, for the moment, he was feeling good again. He had his baby back, and he was focused on keeping it that way. Everything was growing around him. The money was piling up and he was stashing all of the money he was making by hiding it in different places he felt were safe.

After finishing up the business he had to handle, Steve hopped on the freeway and made his way out to Farmington Hills. He met his mother in the parking lot of one of their favorite restaurants. She got out of the car and ran up to Steve and they hugged and kissed each other on the cheeks.

"I've missed you! Where have you been, Mr. Busy?"

"I been working," Steve said as he put his arm around her and walked her into the restaurant. "I been around. I ain't been too far away. Really, I wanted to give you some time to get settled and relax in your new home."

- The Italian hostess seated them at a table toward the back by a window. Although it was gray and rainy outside, the large window let a lot of light into the area they were seated.

Steve's mom smiled at the hostess as she sat down and asked for a glass of white wine. Steve said he was fine with a water. She set down the menus in front of them, and left. "Baby, you know I've been relaxed in my new place. I've been waiting for you to come over so I can cook for you."

He laughed. "I know. I know. I've been kinda busy. I've had a lot going on the last few weeks. I'ma come spend a day with you soon though."

His mother's face got serious. "Is everything ok?" she asked as she reached out and wrapped her hands around his.

"Yeah, everything is ok."

The waitress walked up and introduced herself while setting down the wine and two glasses of water. She was an absolutely gorgeous middle aged woman, maybe Italian or Greek, with beautiful, shiny dark brown hair and deep brown, almost black, eyes. She was probably 45 years old, but looked better than most women in their twenties. She had on a black skirt, with a white button down shirt, unbuttoned to the third button. When she bent down to set down Steve's drink, he couldn't help but notice the round, tan breasts that were pressed together, peeking out of her shirt.

Steve's mother ordered first. She ordered a chicken fettuccini alfredo dish with an antipasto salad for them to share. While his mom ordered, Steve was mesmerized, staring at this waitress's lips and listening to her slight accent. Steve ordered a medium rare ribeye steak with bacon wrapped asparagus and a side of mashed potatoes.

Steve's mom took another sip of her wine, then leaned forward and looked at him, examining him closely like only a mother can do. "Are you still with that girl you were with?"

"I am."

"You ain't had enough of her yet, huh? I'm really not so sure about your choice in women, Steve," she said while tilting her head and squinting one of her eyes at him.

Steve laughed and shook his head. "Why don't you like her, Ma?"

"She's not a likeable chick for a mother that loves her son. You have to understand, Steve. My love for you is unconditional, so I want what's best for you no matter what. No woman will ever be good enough for you in my eyes, but this one is far from what I think you need."

"What does that mean?"

"I'll tell you what that means. It means that I know her kind. She's too sneaky and you deserve better. You are a handsome young man and could have any woman you want. I just wish you would have chose someone better than that skank."

CHAPTER
SIXTY-EIGHT

Steve wished he could tell her what had been going on with them, but there was no way he was going to. All he could do was listen to what she said and take it into consideration. He knew his mom had his best interests in mind, so he tried not to argue. He figured James had told her some things.

"I love her, mom. Like a lot."

"I know, son. And I'm alright with that. I just don't want to see you hurt, and I think she would be the type to hurt you. I know you really like her, but sometimes the things we love, are ultimately not the best thing for us. I told you how I felt years ago and I still feel the same way. You are a very cute couple. Both of you are good looking people, but you have too much of a good heart for her. And people like her . . . they'll take advantage of someone like you, and I just don't like that. Over the years, you have told me more than enough stuff about that girl and I noticed that you've stopped telling me things. I can imagine what you've been going through over there with her."

Steve started to laugh. "Naw, we been working things out and working through things, you know. It hasn't been that bad. She's getting better," he lied.

"Yea, ok. I'll believe it when I see it. I see the stress all in your face. You can't hide that from me."

"Naw, I just been working long hours," he replied as he looked down, playing with his fork a little and looking distracted.

His mom stared at him in silence for some time. "Son, you are aware that I know you better than you think I do, right?"

He laughed and looked up at her. "What's that supposed to mean?"

"You came out of me. What do you think it means?"

Steve sat there silent. He didn't know what to really say.

"I can tell when something is bothering you. I can tell when you are sick. I can tell when you have something on your mind you want to tell me. I can tell a lot." She smiled and took another sip of her wine, giving him a look that signaled that she knew she was right.

Steve squinted his eyes at her. "I'm thinking about marrying Angelia."

"I'm not surprised. I knew that was going to be coming sooner or later. I support whatever decision you make when it comes to your love life. I would never step in the middle of something unless I had to. I love you son. You already know that, and I will love her as my own daughter if that's the route you decide to take. I know you can do way better, though. It is what it is," she said as she folded her arms and leaned back against her chair.

Steve smiled at her, only paying attention to the positive part of what she had to say. "I got a ring already. I'll probably ask her soon. I just wanted to know what you thought about it."

His mom lowered her voice and leaned forward. "I can't control what you do, son. All I can do is pray and hope everything works out for you. You have my blessing. Have you spoke with her parents about it?"

"I plan to, but I haven't just yet."

"I'm sure they will be happy about it . . . well, then again, they may want her to marry a Mexican."

"I should be ok since I'm mixed," he joked and they both laughed.

"Yea, hopefully. Just kidding. You guys have been together for some time now so they understand where you guys are and where you've been. It's obvious they'll support you two."

"Her mom loves me and her dad is cool."

"That's good. So are you thinking about giving me some grandbabies soon?" she asked with a huge grin while lifting her eyebrows.

"Yes, I am," he said as he took a deep breath.

They both laughed.

Steve took a small bag out from next to him and handed it across the table to his mom. The bag contained $20,000, and he asked her to hold onto it for him. She knew he was either selling drugs or scamming banks because he never had money like this before. She was excited about it, but was scared at the same time. She didn't want something bad to happen to him. She wanted to ask him what he had going on because it was getting to be a little much. She had a lot of money put up for him that he had previously given her, in addition to the money James would come and drop off to her every so often. She had good hiding spots for it, but she wanted him to slow down and be careful.

Their meals came and they ate, laughing throughout the entire meal. Steve was having fun spending time with his mom, and knew he needed to take more time to meet with her. After eating and talking for another hour, they went their separate ways. Although his mom didn't like the decision he was making about marrying Angelia, she had expressed her concerns, and Steve was happy she was willing to compromise and work with him. Steve was moving fast and everyone that was close to him was worried about him, but he acted like he had everything under control.

CHAPTER
SIXTY-NINE

fter Steve left his mom, he did more running around, including making a trip all the way to Saginaw and back. Angelia had been sending him pictures of her pussy and tits all day. He almost went off the road watching a video of her playing with a dildo, working at it until she creamed. He was getting excited to get back to her, but he had a few more errands to run before he could go home.

Around 8 o'clock that evening, he walked in the door, tired from the day, but excited to see her. He set his duffle bags of money down on the kitchen counter and looked up. There was Angelia, butt naked, laying on the couch sipping some liquor. "I missed you!" she shouted, running up to him, jumping up, and wrapping her legs around his waist. He kissed her as he held her booty, and pushed one of the duffle bags of money aside to set her down on the counter.

"Missed you too."

They tongue kissed and Steve could taste the liquor in her mouth. He knew that she was tipsy by the way she was kissing him all sloppy. He was loving the attention so he didn't complain. He kissed her back, picked her back up, and carried her to the living room where he sat her down on the back of the couch. She unbuckled his belt and unzipped his pants, realizing that his dick was already hard.

"Turn around, and lean over the couch."

She stood up and leaned over the back of the couch, putting one leg up. Steve pulled one of her ass cheeks to the side as he stuck his dick inside her wet pussy. He started stroking with his pants around his ankles. "This pussy feel so good, baby," he said as he stroked her at a medium pace. Her pussy was getting wetter and wetter and she was moaning louder and louder with each stroke.

"Papi, yes!"

He was holding her waist, mainly pushing himself against her left wall, since he was inside of her at an angle. "Damn, I love this pussy," he moaned as he enjoyed how wet and perfect her pussy felt. The sound of him going in and out of her turned him on even more. "I'ma nut in this pussy, baby," he moaned, pushing himself in deeper and deeper with each stroke.

"Yes, Papi. Give it all to me. Cum in me, Papi," she moaned as she took his firm strokes, matching his speed perfectly with slight backward pressure against each stroke. "You fucking this pussy good, Papi! Don't stop, Papi! I'm going to cum so hard if you keep fucking me like that!"

Steve continued to feel the pressure building inside him as he got ready to burst, but he wanted to wait for her. "Shit, baby, I can't hold it, baby. I'm about to bust!" he groaned as he increased his speed, grabbing her more tightly by the waist.

"Cum in me baby and don't stop, Papi!" Her moans got louder as she felt her body began to tense as an intense orgasm approached the surface. Steve exploded first.

"Arggggh, shit!" he growled as he emptied himself inside her and continued to stroke at the same speed until he was empty. The orgasm took so much out of him he wanted to stop, but he kept pumping away at the same pace. He fought the urge to stop until he felt her pussy grip and release him repeatedly as the orgasm took over her body. She squirted all over him, soaking his hips and legs. She collapsed forward over the back of the couch, and her legs followed behind her causing his dick to slide out. Steve stood with his hands on the back of the couch, looking down at her laying naked on the couch below.

"Damn . . . Papi . . . " she said in between breaths. "That . . . was . . . so good."

"It was like a flood in that pussy. God damn you soaked me." A big drop of semen dropped from the tip of his penis down onto his pants. The rest of it started to flow out of her between her ass cheeks. "Damn, seeing that nut come out of you is so sexy."

"I don't want it to come out of me. Keep it in. Push it back in."

Steve walked around to the couch and got on top of her and put his dick inside of her and started to thrust his hips. He started laughing. "This muthafucka going down. Let me see," he tried putting it back in her, but with how wet she was, it popped out every time he pulled back. "I'm done for now," he said as he pulled out laughing. He draped his body over hers, and laid his head on her shoulder.

"Yeah, that thing like a gummy worm now," she joked, running her fingers against his face.

Steve lifted his head up. "Give me a kiss, sexy ass," he said, sticking his lips out for her to plant one on him. "I told my mom we was about to make her some grandbabies."

"You did? What did she say?"

"She's ready for them. She want some. She wasn't against it at all. I told her we was getting married too."

"No you didn't." Angelia said while she smiled.

"I did," he replied as he got up and made his way to the kitchen to get a rag for Angelia to clean herself up with.

"She is going to kill me," Angelia yelled from the couch.

Steve looked over his shoulder at her and they both laughed together. "Naw, she was cool about it. She's supportive, despite what went on with us in the past."

"That's cool. I can't believe you wasn't scared to tell her that."

"I was, but I wanted to see how she would react. We went to eat today so I was sitting across the table from her when I told her. She kept a normal look on her face and just said that she prays that it'll all work out with us."

"Awww, she's so sweet. We going to be good. In fact, we going to be great," she said, taking the rag from Steve and wiping herself off.

"I agree."

CHAPTER
SEVENTY

S teve carried all his money upstairs, and Angelia followed him. They took all the cash and started running it through the money counter. "What are you going to do with all this?" she asked, smiling.

"Shit, first pay the plug off then we gone live it up. You wanna go shopping?"

"Don't ever ask a woman if she wants to go shopping," she said as she playfully hit him in the arm. "Of course I want to go shopping!"

They both laughed.

"So the guy a couple houses down from us has this boat he wants to sell. It's a nice pontoon boat, fits about 10 people or something. It's a pretty good size I think." He pulled out his phone to show her pictures.

"Ouu, that's nice. You going to get it?"

"Well, I was going to ask you first and see what you thought."

"Yea! Hell yes!" she yelled out in excitement. "The boat is cute. I love it. It looks new!"

"Yea, it's in excellent condition. You can tell he definitely took care of it."

"Do he have some jet skis too?"

"He do. I think he has three of them for sale."

"Yes, Papi. We need those. They would be so much fun. I wanna have sex with you while you driving the jet ski."

He laughed. "That might actually be fun."

"Oh, it for sure will be," she replied, smiling. Steve started texting the guy down the street to ask about his jet skis as well. The guy gave him a deal to take everything. Steve told him that he would bring by $35,000 cash the following day. Angelia was excited and was all over Steve all night. After the excitement about the boat and jet skis died down, Angelia made her way over to the nightstand, and pulled out the bag of coke.

"Remember you said I can get you twisted again," she said, pouring out a little onto the table.

Steve shook his head and smiled. "Yea, I did say that, didn't I?" He walked over to where Angelia was and watched her turn the pile into two small lines.

"You go first this time, Papi," she said, handing him the rolled up bill.

Steve bent over and sniffed the line, getting it all up more efficiently than last time. As he handed Angelia the bill, he could feel the rush start to take over his body. He felt incredible, and immediately felt like doing nothing but having sex. Angelia did her line, then got down on her knees, and started to undo his pants. He was rock hard just from the sensation of him taking down his pants. She started to give him head, and he realized he wasn't frozen this time. He could move like never before. He picked Angelia up after only a minute of her licking his shaft and sucking on his balls, and threw her on the bed. He climbed on top of her and fucked her like an absolute animal, pounding away at her while she climaxed repeatedly. By the time he was done, she fell asleep, snoring loudly.

Steve let her sleep as he did another line then went back into the other room and ran some more money through the counter and organized the room. After an hour he came back into the bedroom, did another line, and slid his dick back inside her, waking her up.

"Oh, you feel that?" he whispered.

"Yes, Papi," she whispered back, arching her back from the side. He was behind her grinding slowly.

"I just did another line," he said as he continued to move in and out of her slowly.

"Without me?"

"Go get one."

"What time is it?"

"One in the morning."

"That's it?"

"Yea, it's still early. Let's turn up."

Angelia was shocked that he was up and ready to go. It was usually the other way around. Steve continued to stroke away at her, groaning, while they were conversing. "Harder," she whispered, reaching behind her and pulling him in closer.

Steve sped up and started going harder and harder. He could feel her warm insides get more and more wet, and he was overwhelmed by the feeling. About two minutes later, he was exploding inside her.

CHAPTER
SEVENTY-ONE

T he next morning, Steve was up early. After getting himself something to eat and throwing on a pair of white basketball shorts and a t-shirt, he counted out $35,000 in all hundred dollar bills, and put them in 4 envelops, $10,000 in 3 of them, and $5,000 in one. He made sure everything looked organized and professional. He even took the time to iron the bills where he needed to flatten them out. He sent the guy down the road a text message, and the guy told him he was ready for him. Steve walked down the street, envelops in hand, and saw the white gentleman standing on his porch waving vigorously at him as he walked up his driveway. The guy was so excited to show him the pontoon and the jet skis. He first took Steve into the garage and showed him the maintenance records for each, all organized into separate folders. Steve was impressed. The man then grabbed two life jackets off a hook, and walked Steve through the back door of his garage and into his back yard.

Steve saw the pontoon sitting up out of the water next to an aluminum dock along with the three jet skis. The man lowered two of the jet skis into the water, and helped Steve get on one. He jumped on the other one, and while floating next to Steve, he explained the controls to him as well as the difference between them. It was a calm day, and the surface of the water looked like a sheet of glass. He could see through the crystal clear water down to the sandy bottom. Steve pushed the ignition and it started right up. They cruised around the lake for about 10 minutes, then the man motioned that he was heading back in. Steve followed him, and couldn't wipe the smile off his face as they got back to the dock. *Angelia is going to love these,* he thought to himself, barely able to wait to take her out on them.

"What do you think?" the guy asked him with a smile.

"Love it, plus they are fast!" Steve said as he stepped back on shore.

The guy laughed. "Yea, it's better to have the power and not need it, you know what I mean?" he said, motioning him to come over to the pontoon. "You still want to check out the boat?"

"Of course! That's what I'm here for." Steve looked over at the pontoon, which was in as good of condition as it looked in the pictures. There were two 200 HP engines off the back of it that really looked brand new. As they stepped on the deck of the pontoon, the guy showed him around. The boat had a blue carpet deck with white seats and blue piping. All the seats shined like the man had just wiped them down with Armor All or some other vinyl protectant. He made sure Steve was aware of all of the storage compartments, and told him that he'd be throwing in the ten orange life jackets with the boat.

"The sheriff is out on this lake every so often, and he does check for life jackets, so you'll want to just leave these in the boat," he said as he closed the top of the seat back on top of them. "Well, hop in the captain's seat, and I'll lower it down," he said. Steve smiled as he sat in the chair and the man pushed them off.

As they cruised around the lake, the man made sure to point out some shallow spots where there were fallen trees in the water which Steve should avoid. Steve couldn't believe how nice this guy was. After docking the boat, the gentleman invited Steve inside, introduced him to his wife, and they sat at his kitchen table. Steve greeted his wife, then, without hesitation, sat the envelops on the table, and said he wanted the pontoon and the jet skis. They smiled at him, and agreed to write him up bills of sale for lower values on each of them, so he could avoid the taxes. Steve really hit it off with this guy, and planned to stop by often.

CHAPTER
SEVENTY-TWO

As Steve was walking back home, his phone started ringing. It was John, Karo's broker. "Hello."

"Hey, Steve. This is John. How are you?"

"I'm good. How are you?"

"I'm doing great, thanks. Hey, I have an office in Dearborn. I was wondering if you had a little time today to sit down and talk. I have some properties that I think you'd be interested in . . . well, I know you'll be interested in them. I actually want to pick these up myself, but I promised Karo that I would get you a great deal to get you up and running."

"Thanks, I appreciate that. Yes, I have some time later today. I'm really ready to make something happen. I was wondering when you'd call."

John laughed. "Yea, I didn't forget about you. This deal I have is probably going to cost you about $300,000 up front and another $200,000 in payments. You're going to need about 250K to fix it up. Can you handle that?"

Steve paused for a moment then replied, "Yea, I think so. That will be cool. I think I can handle that."

"Don't worry. I'm going to be there to help you every step of the way. Bring $300,000 with you today. You're going to want this for sure. It does need a little work, but we've got that all covered. I have people I can refer to you to handle all the renovations."

"Well, what is it?"

"Since this is your first investment, I'll tell you what it is, but next time, I want you to trust me when I tell you that you'll want it."

They both laughed.

"Ok, deal," Steve said.

"A motel. The building has approximately 30 rooms in total. It's a small motel, but it's in a decent area. It's the outdoor style motels, you've probably seen, two levels with no elevators or anything like that. Steve, I want to tell you that there is a huge profit potential in this property. After you put a little work into the rooms, you'll be able to charge $70-80 a night and you'll be all set. You'll need a couple reliable, trustworthy housekeepers. I have a property maintenance team that will handle all mechanical, electrical, HVAC, and plumbing issues. You will be fine. I know this is a big purchase for you, but I wont let you fail. Trust me."

"Yea, as you were talking, I was sitting here like, shit, I don't know anything about running a motel."

"No worries. This is easy stuff man. I have about forty locations similar to the one I'm setting you up with. This location will be a piece of cake for you. I'll show you how to run it. Don't even worry about it. Just get down here around 5 o'clock. I'll text you the address. Cool?"

John was a fast talker, but Steve knew he was in good hands with him.

"Ok, 5 o'clock. I'll be there."

"Great. See you then."

CHAPTER
SEVENTY-THREE

Steve hung up the phone right after he came in the house and closed the garage door behind him. He was excited and nervous at the same time. He walked in and sat down on the couch, giving himself a minute to think.

"Somebody want you to run a motel?" Angelia asked.

"Well, buy one. He wants me to buy one."

"A hotel?" she asked, unable to hide the shock in her voice.

"Yea, it's actually a motel, but it's for sale. It has about 30 rooms. This guy has hotels so he's going to help me with it. You know, walk me through it and all."

"How much is that gonna cost?"

"Like half a million."

Her eyes grew big. "Who got all that?"

Steve didn't seem to get it. He had showed her money, and they just moved into this big house, and she still looked at him like he didn't have any money. In that moment, it became apparent to him that she really didn't know what was going on with him. "We gone figure it out, baby."

"Yea, because you is tripping. That's a lot of money."

Steve sat in silence for a minute before pulling his phone out to text James.

Steve: What you doing?

James: Watering.

Steve: Man, I don't think Angelia look at me like I have the money I have. She still thinks I'm broke or something.

James: What you mean?

Steve: First, let me tell you I'm buying a motel.

James: Hell yea!!! How much?

Steve: About half a million. It has 30 rooms.

James: Hell yea bro! That's what I'm talking about. That sounds like a deal too.

Steve: That's what I'm saying. I told Angelia the same thing.

James: What she say?

Steve: That's a lot of money. You will be paying for that forever. She must not know what's going on.

James: LMAO. She don't bro. Clearly she don't.

Steve: Lol wtf.

James: She from the hood and got a small mind still. If you was buying jewelry, foreign whips, and wearing high end designer shit, she would believe you then. It's sad, but trust me. That's what the problem is for sure.

Steve: Wow, you think she thinks that?

James: Hell yea, for sure. She don't even know what you working with and she sitting right there up under you.

Steve: I think she thinks I'm still working for Unk.

James: Let her think that smh.

Steve: Lol this crazy.

James: Get used to it. People only like the stuff that shines and all that, not knowing that it's a fact that everything that glitters is not gold.

Steve: Facts. I'll talk to you later. I'll probably pull up.

Although Steve was thrown off by the way Angelia responded to him, he still loved and cared for her, so he didn't let it affect him too much. He looked up at Angelia and said, "I'ma be back later on. I'm going to go make a run. I'll be back."

"Well, come upstairs for a second," she said, licking her lips and looking sexy.

"Say less," he said, following her up the stairs. She was wearing some grey spandex shorts, and he could tell she didn't have on any panties. "Damn, that ass so fat," he said, giving it a smack as they hit the top of the stairs.

"And it's all yours too," she said as they made their way into the bedroom. "Lay down. I'ma give you some head before you go."

Steve complied with her request. He never turned Angelia down when she wanted to suck his dick. He pulled his shorts off as he slid up to the middle of the bed. Angelia turned on one of her favorite songs by Tink, and then crawled on top of him. She grabbed his dick and inserted it slowly into her mouth, gently pressing the bottom of his shaft on her tongue. She took her time, going slowly, while staring him in his eyes. She continued to stroke and suck him again and again while slobbing all over it.

"Lick them balls too."

Angelia listened and started licking and sucking gently on both of his balls. As she drew the thin skin that covered his balls into her mouth, it drove him crazy.

"Yes, baby. Just like that. Don't stop stroking that dick," he whispered.

She kept doing what she was doing, then she moved lower and making her way to his asshole. She couldn't quite get to it, so she pushed his legs up and out a little, and then started licking his asshole until it was thoroughly drenched. After a few minutes of that her pussy was dripping wet, and soaking into her grey spandex shorts. She wanted him inside her, but she fought the urge and went back to sucking his dick. Steve could feel himself getting close.

"Stand up. I want you to come on my face."

Steve slid down to the end of the bed and stood up. She dropped to her knees and started sucking his dick like she was in a competition. Steve grabbed the back of her head and started pushing it down into him even though it choked her. Saliva was pouring out of her mouth as she deepthroated his dick until he couldn't hold back any longer.

"Don't stop. I'm bouta cum," he said, taking his dick out of her mouth and spraying ropes of cum all over her face. She stuck her tongue out, catching some of it, while the rest of it shot across her eyes, nose, and lips.

"Arggggggh!!! Shit!" he said as he stroked his dick until it was empty. He patted the last few drops onto the side of her face. "Damn, baby," he said, laughing. "That shit felt good as fuck." He took a couple steps back.

"No, come here," she said, reaching for his dick. She knew it was sensitive, so she gently wrapped her lips around it and sucked out the last few drops without making him jump or tense up. "There you go," she said, popping her mouth off his dick.

"Yea, you marrying me for sure. That shit felt so good," he said, feeling a total sense of relief.

She giggled and blushed. "Glad you liked it, Papi."

CHAPTER
SEVENTY-FOUR

T hey both got in the shower together and Steve got dressed, counted the money out that he needed, and was about to head out when he heard a knock on the door.

"You expecting someone?" he asked, looking at Angelia.

"Yea, Candy wanted to see the new house. Plus, she brought some pregnancy tests for me," she said, smiling.

"You think you pregnant already?"

"I don't know. It's possible though."

"Ayeeeee!" Steve got excited and started doing a little dance.

She giggled and ran downstairs to get the door. Steve brushed his teeth and continued to get himself ready to meet up with John. When he came downstairs, he talked to Candy for a few minutes before heading out the door. He decided to drive the nice car that Karo had given him as a gift. The only thing he didn't like about it was that you didn't see very many of them on the street at all, so people were always stopping and asking him what it was.

It was a nice afternoon, and the sun was shining, still high in the sky. Steve stopped off at the car wash before heading to Detroit. After putting on some tire shine, and drying the car, he took a few steps back and nodded. The longer he had the car, the more he liked it.

He got back in his car, jumped on Telegraph, and headed south with his music turned up. It was rush hour, so there was plenty of traffic, but it was moving along fine. The cars were close to bumper to bumper, but everyone was moving at 55-60 mph, only coming to a stop at a red light every few miles.

Minutes later, his phone rang. It was a private call. Normally, he didn't answer private calls, but for whatever reason he picked up.

"Hello," he answered.

"Why did you block me?"

Steve quickly picked up that it was Shila's voice, and he hung up the phone. He turned his music back up while she continued to call repeatedly. He didn't answer. As he crossed 8 Mile into the city, he got a text message from Angelia. He glanced down and opened it up. It was a picture of three pregnancy tests. All of them showed positive results. He instantly knew what it was and was overwhelmed with happiness. *I'm gonna be a father*, he thought to himself. He dialed Angelia right away.

"We did it, Papi!" she screamed through the phone as she picked up.

Steve laughed as his eyes filled up with tears of joy. "I know. I see! I'm so excited! I don't even know what to say!"

"Yes, me too," she said and then he heard Candy in the background.

"Who's going to be the godmomma?"

They all started laughing.

"We will see. We will see!" Angelia said.

"Well, baby, I'm happy as hell. We gone celebrate later when I get back. Love you."

"You driving still?"

"Yea, it's a lot of traffic on Telegraph."

"Ok, I'll see you later. And yes, we gonna celebrate when you get back. Be safe!"

"Ok, boo," Steve said and hung up the phone. He only had a few more miles until he would be at John's office. He heard a text message come through, and checked his phone. It was from an unknown number. It was a video. He opened it up, and glanced down at it while trying to pay attention to the traffic. He couldn't believe what he saw. It was Angelia sucking someone's dick. The date on the video was only a few months ago. Another text came through.

Shila: It's Shila. Come meet up with me. I have more of these video's for you. I've been telling you she wasn't right for you.

Steve shook his head as he read the text. He glanced back up at the road, only to see a Suburban at a complete stop only 5 feet in front of him with the rest of the traffic stopped in front of it. Steve was going 56 mph. Before his foot could even get halfway to the brake, he slammed into the Suburban. His phone flew out of his hand and his airbags deployed. He laid there slumped over unconscious, bleeding from the mouth.

READERS DISCUSSION QUESTIONS

1. Have you ever assumed a person was broke because of the car they were driving or the clothes they were wearing?
2. What you thinking about Steve's twin cousins?
3. What's your thoughts on Angelia lying about drugs for her father?
4. Should Steve be taking his uncle advice and building credit or all he need is cash?
5. What do you think Shila is up to?
6. How do you feel about the way Angelia reacted to the rapper, Kamozy?
7. Do you think Angelia really love Steve?
8. Should they have got matching tattoos?
9. Were you surprised when Angelia wanted to go to Jon Jon's funeral?
10. What are your thoughts about Steve wanting to marry Angelia?

Lock Down Publications and Ca\$h Presents assisted publishing
packages.

BASIC PACKAGE $499
Editing
Cover Design
Formatting

UPGRADED PACKAGE $800
Typing
Editing
Cover Design
Formatting

ADVANCE PACKAGE $1,200
Typing
Editing
Cover Design
Formatting
Copyright registration
Proofreading
Upload book to Amazon

LDP SUPREME PACKAGE $1,500
Typing
Editing
Cover Design
Formatting
Copyright registration
Proofreading
Set up Amazon account
Upload book to Amazon
Advertise on LDP Amazon and Facebook page

***Other services available upon request. Additional charges may apply
Lock Down Publications
P.O. Box 944
Stockbridge, GA 30281-9998
Phone # 470 303-9761

Submission Guideline

Submit the first three chapters of your completed manuscript to ldpsubmissions@gmail.com, subject line: Your book's title. The manuscript must be in a .doc file and sent as an attachment. Document should be in Times New Roman, double spaced and in size 12 font. Also, provide your synopsis and full contact information. If sending multiple submissions, they must each be in a separate email.

Have a story but no way to send it electronically? You can still submit to LDP/Ca$h Presents. Send in the first three chapters, written or typed, of your completed manuscript to:

LDP: Submissions Dept
Po Box 944
Stockbridge, Ga 30281

DO NOT send original manuscript. Must be a duplicate.

Provide your synopsis and a cover letter containing your full contact information.

Thanks for considering LDP and Ca$h Presents.

NEW RELEASES

THE MURDER QUEENS 3 by MICHAEL GALLON

GORILLAZ IN THE TRENCHES 3 by SAYNOMORE

SALUTE MY SAVAGERY by FUMIYA PAYNE

SUPER GREMLIN by KING RIO

GORILLAZ IN THE BAY V

3X KRAZY III

STRAIGHT BEAST MODE III

De'Kari

KINGPIN KILLAZ IV

STREET KINGS III

PAID IN BLOOD III

CARTEL KILLAZ IV

DOPE GODS III

Hood Rich

SINS OF A HUSTLA II

ASAD

YAYO V

Bred In The Game 2

S. Allen

THE STREETS WILL TALK II

By Yolanda Moore

SON OF A DOPE FIEND III

HEAVEN GOT A GHETTO III

SKI MASK MONEY III

By Renta

LOYALTY AIN'T PROMISED III

By Keith Williams

I'M NOTHING WITHOUT HIS LOVE II

SINS OF A THUG II

TO THE THUG I LOVED BEFORE II

IN A HUSTLER I TRUST II

By Monet Dragun

QUIET MONEY IV

EXTENDED CLIP III

THUG LIFE IV

By **Trai'Quan**

THE STREETS MADE ME IV

By **Larry D. Wright**

IF YOU CROSS ME ONCE III

ANGEL V

By **Anthony Fields**

THE STREETS WILL NEVER CLOSE IV

By **K'ajji**

HARD AND RUTHLESS III

KILLA KOUNTY IV

By **Khufu**

MONEY GAME III

By **Smoove Dolla**

JACK BOYS VS DOPE BOYS IV

A GANGSTA'S QUR'AN V

COKE GIRLZ II

COKE BOYS II

LIFE OF A SAVAGE V

CHI'RAQ GANGSTAS V

SOSA GANG III

BRONX SAVAGES II

BODYMORE KINGPINS II

BLOOD OF A GOON II

By **Romell Tukes**

MURDA WAS THE CASE III

Elijah R. Freeman

AN UNFORESEEN LOVE IV

BABY, I'M WINTERTIME COLD III

By **Meesha**

QUEEN OF THE ZOO III

By **Black Migo**

CONFESSIONS OF A JACKBOY III

By **Nicholas Lock**

KING KILLA II

By **Vincent "Vitto" Holloway**

BETRAYAL OF A THUG III

By **Fre$h**

THE BIRTH OF A GANGSTER III

By **Delmont Player**

TREAL LOVE II

By **Le'Monica Jackson**

FOR THE LOVE OF BLOOD III

By **Jamel Mitchell**

RAN OFF ON DA PLUG II

By **Paper Boi Rari**

HOOD CONSIGLIERE III

By **Keese**

PRETTY GIRLS DO NASTY THINGS II

By **Nicole Goosby**

LOVE IN THE TRENCHES II

By **Corey Robinson**

IT'S JUST ME AND YOU II

By Ah'Million

FOREVER GANGSTA III

By Adrian Dulan

THE COCAINE PRINCESS IX

SUPER GREMLIN II

By King Rio

CRIME BOSS II

Playa Ray

LOYALTY IS EVERYTHING III

Molotti

HERE TODAY GONE TOMORROW II

By Fly Rock

REAL G'S MOVE IN SILENCE II

By Von Diesel

GRIMEY WAYS IV

By Ray Vinci

SALUTE MY SAVAGERY II

By Fumiya Payne

<u>Available Now</u>

RESTRAINING ORDER **I & II**

By **CA$H & Coffee**

LOVE KNOWS NO BOUNDARIES **I II & III**

By **Coffee**

RAISED AS A GOON I, II, III & IV

BRED BY THE SLUMS I, II, III

BLAST FOR ME I & II

ROTTEN TO THE CORE I II III

A BRONX TALE I, II, III

DUFFLE BAG CARTEL I II III IV V VI

HEARTLESS GOON I II III IV V

A SAVAGE DOPEBOY I II

DRUG LORDS I II III

CUTTHROAT MAFIA I II

KING OF THE TRENCHES

By **Ghost**

LAY IT DOWN **I & II**

LAST OF A DYING BREED I II

BLOOD STAINS OF A SHOTTA I & II III

By **Jamaica**

LOYAL TO THE GAME I II III

LIFE OF SIN I, II III

By **TJ & Jelissa**

BLOODY COMMAS I & II

SKI MASK CARTEL I II & III

KING OF NEW YORK I II,III IV V

RISE TO POWER I II III

COKE KINGS I II III IV V

BORN HEARTLESS I II III IV

KING OF THE TRAP I II

By **T.J. Edwards**

IF LOVING HIM IS WRONG…I & II

LOVE ME EVEN WHEN IT HURTS I II III

By **Jelissa**

WHEN THE STREETS CLAP BACK I & II III

THE HEART OF A SAVAGE I II III IV

MONEY MAFIA I II

LOYAL TO THE SOIL I II III

By **Jibril Williams**

A DISTINGUISHED THUG STOLE MY HEART I II & III

LOVE SHOULDN'T HURT I II III IV

RENEGADE BOYS I II III IV

PAID IN KARMA I II III

SAVAGE STORMS I II III

AN UNFORESEEN LOVE I II III

BABY, I'M WINTERTIME COLD I II

By **Meesha**

A GANGSTER'S CODE I &, II III

A GANGSTER'S SYN I II III

THE SAVAGE LIFE I II III

CHAINED TO THE STREETS I II III

BLOOD ON THE MONEY I II III

A GANGSTA'S PAIN I II III

By J-Blunt

PUSH IT TO THE LIMIT

By **Bre' Hayes**

BLOOD OF A BOSS **I, II, III, IV, V**

I LOVE YOU TO DEATH

By **Destiny J**

I RIDE FOR MY HITTA

I STILL RIDE FOR MY HITTA

By **Misty Holt**

LOVE & CHASIN' PAPER

By **Qay Crockett**

TO DIE IN VAIN

SINS OF A HUSTLA

By **ASAD**

BROOKLYN HUSTLAZ

By **Boogsy Morina**

BROOKLYN ON LOCK I & II

By **Sonovia**

GANGSTA CITY

By **Teddy Duke**

A DRUG KING AND HIS DIAMOND I & II III

A DOPEMAN'S RICHES

HER MAN, MINE'S TOO I, II

CASH MONEY HO'S

THE WIFEY I USED TO BE I II

PRETTY GIRLS DO NASTY THINGS

By Nicole Goosby

TRAPHOUSE KING **I II & III**

KINGPIN KILLAZ I II III

STREET KINGS I II

PAID IN BLOOD **I II**

CARTEL KILLAZ I II III

DOPE GODS I II

By **Hood Rich**

LIPSTICK KILLAH **I, II, III**

CRIME OF PASSION I II & III

FRIEND OR FOE I II III

By **Mimi**

STEADY MOBBN' **I, II, III**

THE STREETS STAINED MY SOUL I II III

By **Marcellus Allen**

WHO SHOT YA **I, II, III**

SON OF A DOPE FIEND I II

HEAVEN GOT A GHETTO I II

SKI MASK MONEY I II

Renta

GORILLAZ IN THE BAY **I II III IV**

TEARS OF A GANGSTA I II

3X KRAZY I II

STRAIGHT BEAST MODE I II

DE'KARI

TRIGGADALE I II III

MURDAROBER WAS THE CASE I II

Elijah R. Freeman

GOD BLESS THE TRAPPERS I, II, III

THESE SCANDALOUS STREETS I, II, III

FEAR MY GANGSTA I, II, III IV, V

THESE STREETS DON'T LOVE NOBODY I, II

BURY ME A G I, II, III, IV, V

A GANGSTA'S EMPIRE I, II, III, IV

THE DOPEMAN'S BODYGAURD I II

THE REALEST KILLAZ I II III

THE LAST OF THE OGS I II III

Tranay Adams

THE STREETS ARE CALLING

Duquie Wilson

MARRIED TO A BOSS I II III

By Destiny Skai & Chris Green

KINGZ OF THE GAME I II III IV V VI VII

CRIME BOSS

Playa Ray

SLAUGHTER GANG I II III

RUTHLESS HEART I II III

By Willie Slaughter

FUK SHYT

By Blakk Diamond

DON'T F#CK WITH MY HEART I II

By Linnea

ADDICTED TO THE DRAMA I II III

IN THE ARM OF HIS BOSS II

By Jamila

YAYO I II III IV

A SHOOTER'S AMBITION I II

THE STREETS NEVER LET GO I II III

By Robert Baptiste

NEW TO THE GAME I II III

MONEY, MURDER & MEMORIES I II III

By **Malik D. Rice**

LIFE OF A SAVAGE I II III IV

A GANGSTA'S QUR'AN I II III IV

MURDA SEASON I II III

GANGLAND CARTEL I II III

CHI'RAQ GANGSTAS I II III IV

KILLERS ON ELM STREET I II III

JACK BOYZ N DA BRONX I II III

A DOPEBOY'S DREAM I II III

JACK BOYS VS DOPE BOYS I II III

COKE GIRLZ

COKE BOYS

SOSA GANG I II

BRONX SAVAGES

BODYMORE KINGPINS

BLOOD OF A GOON

By Romell Tukes

LOYALTY AIN'T PROMISED I II

By Keith Williams

QUIET MONEY I II III

THUG LIFE I II III

EXTENDED CLIP I II

A GANGSTA'S PARADISE

By **Trai'Quan**

THE STREETS MADE ME I II III

By **Larry D. Wright**

THE ULTIMATE SACRIFICE I, II, III, IV, V, VI

KHADIFI

IF YOU CROSS ME ONCE I II

ANGEL I II III IV

IN THE BLINK OF AN EYE

By **Anthony Fields**

THE LIFE OF A HOOD STAR

By **Ca$h & Rashia Wilson**

THE STREETS WILL NEVER CLOSE I II III

By **K'ajji**

CREAM I II III

THE STREETS WILL TALK

By **Yolanda Moore**

NIGHTMARES OF A HUSTLA I II III

By **King Dream**

CONCRETE KILLA I II III

VICIOUS LOYALTY I II III

By **Kingpen**

HARD AND RUTHLESS I II

MOB TOWN 251

THE BILLIONAIRE BENTLEYS I II III

REAL G'S MOVE IN SILENCE

By **Von Diesel**

GHOST MOB

Stilloan Robinson

MOB TIES I II III IV V VI

SOUL OF A HUSTLER, HEART OF A KILLER I II

GORILLAZ IN THE TRENCHES I II III

By SayNoMore

BODYMORE MURDERLAND I II III

THE BIRTH OF A GANGSTER I II

By Delmont Player

FOR THE LOVE OF A BOSS

By C. D. Blue

MOBBED UP I II III IV

THE BRICK MAN I II III IV V

THE COCAINE PRINCESS I II III IV V VI VII VIII

SUPER GREMLIN

By King Rio

KILLA KOUNTY I II III IV

By Khufu

MONEY GAME I II

By Smoove Dolla

A GANGSTA'S KARMA I II III

By FLAME

KING OF THE TRENCHES I II III

by **GHOST & TRANAY ADAMS**

QUEEN OF THE ZOO I II

By **Black Migo**

GRIMEY WAYS I II III

By Ray Vinci

XMAS WITH AN ATL SHOOTER

By Ca$h & Destiny Skai

KING KILLA

By Vincent "Vitto" Holloway

BETRAYAL OF A THUG I II

By Fre$h

THE MURDER QUEENS I II III

By Michael Gallon

TREAL LOVE

By Le'Monica Jackson

FOR THE LOVE OF BLOOD I II

By Jamel Mitchell

HOOD CONSIGLIERE I II

By Keese

PROTÉGÉ OF A LEGEND I II III

LOVE IN THE TRENCHES

By Corey Robinson

BORN IN THE GRAVE I II III

By Self Made Tay

MOAN IN MY MOUTH

By XTASY

TORN BETWEEN A GANGSTER AND A GENTLEMAN

By J-BLUNT & Miss Kim

LOYALTY IS EVERYTHING I II

Molotti

HERE TODAY GONE TOMORROW

By Fly Rock

PILLOW PRINCESS

By S. Hawkins

NAÏVE TO THE STREETS
WOMEN LIE MEN LIE I II III
GIRLS FALL LIKE DOMINOS
STACK BEFORE YOU SPURLGE
FIFTY SHADES OF SNOW I II III
By A. Roy Milligan
SALUTE MY SAVAGERY

By Fumiya Payne

BOOKS BY LDP'S CEO, CA$H

Printed in the USA
CPSIA information can be obtained
at www.ICGtesting.com
LVHW050459090823
754680LV00003BA/160